'Do you perceive embarking in another career direction?'

She met the queries head-on. 'Such as?'

'Marriage.'

'Doubtful. Why repeat a mistake?'

'We agree Christina needs a mother. I'm proposing you take on that role.'

It got her attention, as it was meant to do.

'As my wife,' Manolo added, to clarify any misunderstanding.

She just looked at him. 'You're insane.'

'Am I?' He trapped her gaze.

Lovers and friends. Just the mere thought of having him as a lover sent her emotions spiralling out of control.

Helen Bianchin was born in New Zealand, and travelled to Australia before marrying her Italian-born husband. After three years they moved, returned to New Zealand with their daughter, had two sons, then resettled in Australia. Encouraged by friends to recount anecdotes of her years as a tobacco sharefarmer's wife living in an Italian community, Helen began setting words on paper, and her first novel was published in 1975. An animal lover, she says her terrier and Persian cat regard her study as much theirs as hers.

Recent titles by the same author:

IN THE SPANIARD'S BED
THE PREGNANCY PROPOSAL

THE SPANIARD'S BABY BARGAIN

BY
HELEN BIANCHIN

All the characters in this book have no existence outside the imagination of the author, and have no relation whatsoever to anyone bearing the same name or names. They are not even distantly inspired by any individual known or unknown to the author, and all the incidents are pure invention.

First published in Great Britain 2004
Harlequin Mills & Boon Limited,
Eton House, 18-24 Paradise Road, Richmond, Surrey TW9 1SR

© Helen Bianchin 2004

ISBN 0 263 83751 3

Set in Times Roman 10½ on 13 pt.
01-0704-34484

Printed and bound in Spain
by Litografía Rosés, S.A., Barcelona

CHAPTER ONE

MANOLO paid the cab driver, collected his valise, and mounted the few steps to the main entrance of his harbour-front mansion set high in Sydney's suburban Point Piper.

The front door opened before he could extract his keys.

'Good evening, Manolo. Welcome home.'

Some welcome, he qualified silently. His home in an uproar, the third nanny in as many months about to walk, and, God help him, a media journalist and cameraman due to descend in less than an hour to begin a weekend documentary he'd agreed to do over a month ago.

'Santos,' he acknowledged to the ex-chef who'd served as his live-in factotum for several years, and offered a grim smile as he entered the spacious foyer. 'What in hell happened this time?'

'Little Christina is teething,' the manservant relayed. 'The nanny resents her own lack of sleep.'

Manolo raked restless fingers through his hair. 'Where is she?'

'Packing,' Santos declared with succinct cynicism.

'You've arranged a replacement?'

'Tried to. Unfortunately our record with nannies elicited the response the agency has no one sufficiently qualified to fill the position until next week.'

'Mierda.' The oath escaped with soft vehemence.

Santos lifted one eyebrow. 'My sentiments exactly.'

He'd deal with it. Have to. There was no other option. 'Maria?' The house-cleaner came in five days a week, but left each day at four to care for her large family.

'She assures she can give an extra few hours to help out.'

'Any messages?' It was merely a general query, for anything important reached him via cellphone or email.

'I've put the mail and messages in the usual place. Dinner will be ready in half an hour.'

Time to shave, shower, dress, then eat before he was due to greet the media crew. But first he needed to see his young daughter, deal with the departing nanny.

He stifled a grimace, and resisted the temptation to roll his shoulders. Hell. The last thing he felt like doing after a long international flight was to exchange small talk with a media representative.

What on earth had possessed him to agree to this *personal profile* documentary in the first place? Ah, yes, the stipulation it would showcase his favourite charity. Plus the fact the interview would be conducted by Ariane Celeste...a petite ash-blonde woman in her late twenties, whose television persona intrigued him.

The nanny was on her way down the wide curving staircase as he reached the first step, and he paused, waiting for her to draw level.

She was young, too young, he decided as he viewed her set features. 'Would a bonus persuade you to stay on until I can arrange a replacement?'

'No.'

He could press the point, imply she was obligated to give a week's notice, redress his legal right as an employer...but dammit, he wasn't sure he wanted someone harbouring unwillingness and resentment to care for Christina.

'Santos will order a cab. My cheque will be sent to the agency.'

'Thanks.'

Her brief, almost impolite response incurred a dark glance from Santos, which Manolo met and dismissed in silence as he turned and ascended the stairs.

The volume of his daughter's voice increased as he reached the upper level, and a hand closed over his heart and squeezed a little as he entered the nursery.

The small face was red with the force of her cries, the dark hair damp from exertion. Worse, she'd soiled her nappy, and her legs were pumping in active protest.

'*Por Dios.*' The soft imprecation brought a second's silence, followed immediately by louder cries that rapidly dissolved into hiccups.

'Shh, *pequeña*,' he soothed as he lifted her from the cot and cradled her close. 'Let's tend to you, hmm?'

With competent movements he did just that, trying to coax the distress from those tear-filled dark eyes.

His, he accepted silently. But unmistakably the child of his late wife…a woman who'd connived to bear his name by fair means or foul. And had succeeded, he determined grimly, by deliberately tampering with a prophylactic so she could fall pregnant with his child.

It didn't sit well, even now, that the sole reason for the pregnancy had been to extract a large financial settlement from him and a meal ticket for life.

The thought of a child of his being a victim of its mother's scheming was unconscionable. He'd made Yvonne a handsome offer her avaricious mind wouldn't refuse. Subject to his paternity being proved by DNA, they'd enter the shortest marriage in history to give him legal parental rights, she'd agree to give up the child into his sole custody, then he'd initiate divorce proceedings.

All tied up in a legal contract, on which she had signed her name with a speed that had sickened him.

If there was such a thing as divine justice, he reflected, Yvonne had reaped it. A month after Christina's birth he'd been in New York when he received the news Yvonne had died in a fatal car accident late at night after attending a party. The man with her had shared a similar fate.

He'd taken the next flight home and picked up the pieces, dealt with the media rumours, a departing nanny and employed another.

The second of four in five months, he conceded with grim cynicism. The longest any one of them had stayed was seven weeks.

The small babe in his arms gave a shuddering cry and latched onto her tiny fist.

'Hungry, *pequeña*?' Her needs held importance over his own, and he crossed to the large storage cabinet, opened it, checked the small refrigerator, witnessed several bottles of made-up formula and breathed a sigh of relief.

A minute in the microwave, and the temperature was right.

He sank into the rocking chair and began feeding his daughter…not a moment too soon, given the desperation with which she took the bottle.

'Need any help?'

Manolo met Santos' measured gaze, lifted one eyebrow in silent cynicism, and offered with droll humour, 'What do you suggest?'

They shared a long history and unconditional trust. A friendship, despite the employer-employee relationship, that went back to the days when he'd become streetwise from an early age in a tough New York neighbourhood where self-survival was a priority. It wasn't a youth he was particularly proud of, but one that had shaped him into the man he was today.

Hard-edged, ruthless, a risk-taker who'd worked in three jobs, studied, and existed on minimum sleep to gain millionaire status in his early twenties. Something he'd multiplied almost a thousand-fold over the past fifteen years.

No one dared toy with him without paying the price. Love wasn't an emotion he had been familiar with during any part of his life.

Manolo checked his watch and suppressed a grimace. Fifteen minutes to shave, shower and eat wasn't enough. So he'd be late.

'I'll welcome the media duo when they arrive, show them to their rooms, offer them a drink,' Santos declared smoothly. 'That'll allow you a timely entrance.'

Home security was a necessary addition to any rich man's property, but the high, elaborate wrought-iron gates attached to equally high concrete walls, the mounted surveillance camera…

Overkill, or did Manolo del Guardo have reason for such hi-tech protection?

'Who is this guy? Croesus?'

'Not quite.'

'Done your homework, huh?' came the nonchalant

response as the car drew to a halt in front of the imposing gates.

'Can you recall a time when I didn't?'

Ariane knew exactly who Manolo del Guardo was. She'd compiled a file on him. Together with a detailed list of questions…some of which, she conceded, were guaranteed to evoke a strong, even heated response.

However, that was the purpose of her interview. To dig beneath the surface and provide an insightful and, at times, provocative look at the lives of those who had risen to notoriety and fame.

Not necessarily together, but in the case of Manolo del Guardo there was a connection to both.

'OK,' Tony initiated as he undid his safety belt. 'Let's go do this.'

State-of-the-art security, Ariane corrected as she observed Tony present his ID tag and driver's licence for verification.

She was aware of a disembodied voice seconds before Tony slid in behind the wheel, then the gates opened with electronic precision.

Summer daylight-saving allowed a view of the curved driveway with its magnificent floral borders, lush, manicured lawn, sculpted shrubs and topiary.

A beautiful foreground to showcase the del Guardo mansion, Ariane conceded, suppressing her surprise. Information she'd gleaned revealed Manolo del Guardo had bought the property for its panoramic view of the Sydney harbour, gutted the existing home, and rebuilt.

A château, designed in the classical French Napoleonic style, she perceived, and not something reflecting his Spanish roots.

She would kill to capture it on film. Except one of the stipulations set down in granting this documentary was no external photographs of the house were to be shot. Internal only, and/or featuring the view, with the proviso each shot required Manolo del Guardo's approval.

Who did he think he was? *God?*

'Where,' Tony attempted mildly as the SUV slowed to a crawl close to the main entrance, 'do you suggest I should park?'

At that moment the huge, elaborately carved double wooden doors swung open and a formally attired manservant descended the few steps.

'Good evening. My name is Santos.' The voice was clipped and bore a slight accent. 'If you would drive to the service entry.' He indicated the direction with a sweep of his arm. 'You'll find the door unlocked. I'll meet you there. You can unload your gear and store it in the storage room.'

Without a further word he retraced his steps and closed the massive front doors behind him.

'Should we assume we've been subtly made aware of our place?' Tony arched as he eased the SUV round the side of the house.

It took only minutes to transfer their equipment indoors, then, overnight bags in hand, they followed Santos through to the main foyer.

Priceless travertine marble floors, expensive oriental rugs, *objets d'art*, original oil paintings, luxurious furnishings, high vaulted ceilings, a breathtaking crystal chandelier, and a wide curving double staircase leading to an upper gallery level. The balustrade was a work of art in itself, its black wrought-iron filigree pattern capped by dark mahogany.

No doubt all the rooms reflected similar accoutrements, and Ariane complimented his taste…or should that be his interior decorator?

'I'll show you to your rooms,' Santos informed as he proceeded towards the staircase. 'Mr del Guardo will meet with you in fifteen minutes.' He indicated an open doorway to his left. 'Please assemble in the informal lounge.'

Formal, informal…casual living? It figured in a mansion this size.

Assemble? There were only two of them, for heaven's sake…hardly a media horde.

The stair-treads were marble, extending onto a tiled foyer and a circular gallery.

Private quarters to the right, guest suites to the left?

The reverse, she determined as she followed Santos to a suite that topped any luxury hotel accommodation.

Muted pastels blended to perfection, exquisite mahogany furniture, sage-green carpet. A large bed, small desk, telephone, television.

Tony's suite was situated close by, and equalled her own, although the colour scheme employed various shades of coffee and cream.

'I'm sure you'll be very comfortable.'

Tony's soft whistle of appreciation resulted in a wry smile from Manolo del Guardo's factotum. 'I'll leave you to confer and unpack. Refreshments will be served in the informal lounge.'

'All this,' Tony said quietly as soon as Santos had disappeared out of earshot, 'screams serious money.'

'The early gathering of which is shrouded in mystery,' Ariane reminded.

'A fact you intend to uncover?'

'If I can.' She checked her watch, and spared the cameraman a faint smile. 'Eleven minutes, and counting. See you in ten.'

Unpacking wasn't an issue, for she travelled light, necessities scaled down to the minimum, and as to freshening up…a quick glance in the *en suite* mirror revealed her hair was tidy, the soft colour on her lips intact.

The muted burr of her cellphone triggered the usual stab of irritation. Right on time, she perceived grimly, as the call went to message-bank.

Common sense warned she should ignore it. Advice given by her lawyer, endorsed by the legal court, and enforced by the restraining order in place against a man who'd succeeded in making her life a living hell through his delusional psychotic behaviour.

A man who'd kept such traits well-hidden during their brief courtship, she reflected, remembering vividly when they had begun to emerge on their honeymoon.

His desire for children had matched her own. What she hadn't expected was the level of his disappointment when she didn't immediately fall pregnant. He had belittled her ability as a lover, damned her with harsh accusations as to her possible sterility...a fact soon endorsed by the medical professionals.

Roger's physical rage at the diagnosis was the last straw, and Ariane had packed her belongings, moved into an apartment, and begun divorce proceedings.

Instead of removing her from the line of fire, it had pitched her right into it as her life became a nightmare, with confrontations, abusive calls...

Calls which had continued with sickening regularity over time, despite a divorce decree, which merely heightened Roger's refusal to move on.

Fat chance, she reflected grimly.

Admittedly the confrontations had subsided, but the text messages were a constant, despite her changing her cellphone number numerous times, opting for private listing, yet still he managed to bypass her security measures.

On this occasion the text message was brief, in the

shorthand favoured by seasoned SMS users, but nevertheless it sent a chill shiver down her spine.

He knew where she was, who she was with, and the duration of her stay. *How?* Almost as soon as she asked herself the question, the answer followed…it wouldn't be too difficult if he employed devious means and managed to bypass the television company's security.

Something Roger could manage with one hand tied behind his back.

'Ready?'

The sound of Tony's voice intruded, and she offered him a slight smile, then collected a slim briefcase. 'Yes.'

The job at hand demanded her concentration, and she preceded the cameraman into the hallway, choosing a leisurely pace to the head of the staircase before descending to the ground floor.

'To the right,' Tony indicated, and she sent him a nod in acknowledgement.

'Got it.'

Focus, she demanded silently as she switched mind-set and summoned a polite, businesslike smile.

Manolo del Guardo.

She'd seen photographs of the man in newspapers and the social pages of glossy magazines. Read his official biographical details, and scraped the surface of the unofficial.

Yet nothing prepared her for the man's physical presence.

Or for her own reaction to him.

Tall, with the build of a warrior...albeit a well-dressed one in dark trousers and an equally dark shirt. Hand-tooled shoes, unless she was mistaken, an expensive watch visible beneath rolled-back cuffs.

Dark, well-groomed hair, dark, almost black eyes, and broad sculpted facial features that owed much to his Spanish heritage.

And something else she couldn't define. A man who'd seen much, weathered more, and developed an impenetrable barrier against any intrusion in his personal life?

Whatever, he resembled a predator indolently at ease. A dangerous one, she perceived, and she fought off the chill shiver threatening to slip down her spine as he moved towards her.

'Ariane Celeste.' It seemed important to get the first word in ahead of him. She summoned a brisk smile as she indicated the cameraman at her side. 'Tony di Marco.'

She extended her hand, and resisted the temptation to hold her breath as he took it firmly within his own, held, then released it before extending the courtesy to the cameraman.

The sizzling heat fizzing through her veins came as a surprise. Accompanied by sensation spiralling from deep within, the combination wasn't something she coveted, and she deliberately banked it down, capped it, and adopted her usual businesslike façade.

'I'd like to thank you for inviting us into your home.'

One eyebrow slanted in musing query. 'The proposal was your own.' The words held an intonation that was pure New York.

Statistics revealed he'd been born to a single mother in the Bronx who raised him until his mid-teens, when cancer claimed her, leaving him to survive alone.

His success story was legend. His philanthropist interests well-tabled. In his late thirties, he owned homes in various capital cities around the world. Including Sydney, which for the past five years he'd chosen as his base.

'One you agreed to,' Ariane responded with polite civility, and glimpsed his faint smile.

'There were conditions, if you recall?'

'Of course. I intend to abide by them.'

Manolo del Guardo inclined his head, then he swept an arm towards a clutch of buttoned leather chairs. 'Please, take a seat. Can I offer you something to drink? Alcohol, coffee, tea?'

Coffee, definitely. The aroma of an expensive fresh brew teased her senses. 'Coffee, black,' she requested. 'One sugar.'

'Ditto,' Tony added.

Manolo del Guardo's dark gaze speared her own,

and her chin tilted fractionally. 'I'll reserve the al-cohol for tomorrow evening,' she ventured sweetly. 'I may need it by then.'

Was that a glimmer of a smile, or did the edge of his mouth merely effect a faint twitch?

'You anticipate I'll be a difficult subject?'

Oh, he was smooth. Too smooth. And three steps ahead of her.

'It's my job to provide an interesting, informative and thought-provoking documentary detailing your rise through the ranks to highlight the man you've become today.'

'Thirty minutes in the life of...' he indicated. 'Ed-ited from twenty-four hours of film?'

He did cynical amusement well. But then, so did she. 'I would hope to wrap it up in twelve.'

Manolo del Guardo poured the coffee, added sugar, and handed them out, then he took a chair opposite.

'Perhaps, Ariane, you will provide me with an overview of the questions you intend to ask?'

The sound of her name on his lips caused goose-pimples in the most unlikely places. For heaven's sake, she mentally chastised in self-disgust. *Get a grip.*

With deliberate control she extracted two printed copies from her briefcase, handed him one, attached her copy to a clipboard, then sat with pen poised.

'A verbal overview, Ariane.'

There they were again...more goose-pimples. How

would he react if she dismissed convention and called him *Manolo*?

Damn him. If he was needling her... 'You prefer the informality of a first-name basis?' She could play, too.

'As we're going to be in each other's company fairly constantly over the next two days, relaxed informality will ease any subsequent tension, don't you think?'

Yeah, right. No one relaxed in the presence of a predator, animal or human. And instinct warned Manolo del Guardo was dangerous in either guise.

'It's my understanding you were given a written overview prior to agreeing to the documentary.' She tempered her words with a conciliatory smile. 'However, I'm quite willing to recap.'

Which she did, with a succinct professionalism that didn't falter. When she was done, she met his studied gaze with equanimity. 'Is that sufficiently extensive?'

'Yes. For now.' He rose to his feet in one fluid movement. 'If you'll excuse me? I have matters to attend to. Please help yourself to more coffee. Feel free to enjoy television in the entertainment room situated in the room adjoining this. There is a selection of DVDs, or cable if you prefer.' He inclined his head to Tony, then turned towards Ariane and lingered a little long. 'Santos will serve breakfast at eight.'

He moved from the room with the ease of a man in command of the situation.

Dangerous, Ariane accorded silently. Definitely dangerous.

'Do you imagine that gives us carte blanche?'

Tony, ever the satirist.

'You're kidding, right?' Ariane crossed to the chiffonier. 'More coffee?' She refilled her cup, added sugar, and turned to face the cameraman.

She'd worked with him on various assignments in the past, and they'd formed an easy camaraderie that had its base in friendship and a mutual respect for each other's talent.

'No, thanks.' He checked his watch. 'Anything you want to go over before we hit the sack?'

Ariane surveyed him over the rim of her cup. 'I want this to be hard-edged, not a piece of condescending fluff,' she specified, and glimpsed his faint smile.

'You don't do *fluff*.'

No, she didn't. What was more, she'd earned a reputation for being able to dig deep and get the facts.

So why did she have this niggling feeling it would be Manolo del Guardo who controlled the interview, and not her?

She finished her coffee and returned the cup and saucer to the chiffonier.

'OK, let's get an early night.' Tomorrow she needed to be bright-eyed and mentally alert.

Instinct warned parrying words with Manolo del Guardo would be the antithesis of a walk in the park.

So, she'd go over her notes one more time, explore a few angles and fine-tune some of the questions.

Ariane preceded Tony from the room and walked at his side as they ascended the stairs to the upper floor.

'See you at breakfast.' Tony offered a slow smile as they paused outside their adjacent suites. 'Relax. It'll be fine.'

She shot him a quizzical glance. 'Breakfast?'

The smile widened. 'Sleep well.'

Usually she did, but a leisurely shower followed by an hour with her notes did little to ease the faint edge of tension, and she switched off the bedside lamp in a determined bid to gain a good night's rest.

In the darkness her thought-train remained with Manolo del Guardo and the possible scenarios the next day would bring.

It was impossible not to dwell on the man himself…the sheer physicality of his height and breadth of shoulder, raw-boned facial features, a strong jawline and a sensual mouth.

As to her electrifying reaction to his presence…what the hell was that?

CHAPTER TWO

ARIANE woke bathed in sweat, still caught up in a disturbing dream so hauntingly vivid it left her on the brink of fear. There had been the distant cry of a baby, and she wasn't able to distinguish whether it belonged in the dream or was seated in reality.

She lay still for a few minutes, checked the time, and opted to shower and dress. It was early, but it would give her an opportunity to go over Manolo del Guardo's personal profile, check details she'd highlighted in order to delve more deeply into his past, then she'd appear downstairs at the appointed time for breakfast.

Alone, she determined as she entered the dining room an hour and a half later. The table was set for one, and an elegant chiffonier held a covered dish, a carafe of steaming coffee, and a jug of orange juice.

The morning newspaper lay folded within reach, and she scanned the newsprint as she ate, then when she was done she returned to her suite to freshen up and gather her notes.

Five minutes to *showtime*, she determined as she entered the informal lounge, and found Tony checking the audio equipment. The video recorder was set up in readiness.

'Hi.' He glanced up from the task in hand. 'Sleep well?'

'OK.' There was no point in admitting to a restless night. 'You?'

'Fine. Woke early, did a few warm-ups in the gym, then swam a few lengths of the indoor lap pool.' He offered a grin. 'Santos granted permission.'

A gym? It figured. As to an indoor lap pool...she might need to avail herself of it in order to cool off after a day parrying words with Manolo del Guardo!

'I'm impressed.'

Tony raised a quizzical eyebrow. 'With my early-morning zest for exercise?'

'That, too.'

His soft laugh brought an answering smile, only to have it die as the soft burr of her cellphone signalled an incoming text message. Business...had to be. Yet it didn't stop her stomach muscles clenching with nervous tension as she read the script.

Is he good in bed, darling?

Roger. Stepping up his ongoing campaign to stalk and harass. Didn't he have anything better to do?

Stupid question. She was his obsession, the focus of his delusion. And he was clever...sufficiently so to fool the legal system.

He intruded into her everyday life. Appearing wherever she happened to be, silent but *there*...

among the occupants of a café where she happened to meet a friend for coffee; a restaurant where she chose to dine; in a supermarket; the cinema. On the fringes, never making direct contact, but ensuring she was aware of his presence.

It was irritating, maddening…as he meant it to be.

'Problems?'

Ariane deleted the message. 'Nothing I can't handle.'

Tony didn't appear convinced, and she sent him a reassuring smile. 'Really.' She spared her watch a glance. 'We did say nine, didn't we?'

'Indeed.' The faintly accented drawl held a degree of cynical humour. 'Although I was unaware of the need for a strict timetable.'

Their host and the subject of the interview stood just inside the doorway, looking totally at ease in black tailored trousers and white chambray shirt with the top few buttons left undone and cuffs turned back.

He moved with the lithe grace of a jungle cat, for she hadn't heard a sound.

Lean-hipped, broad-framed and tall, Manolo del Guardo cut a dynamic figure. Raw-boned facial features, a sensuous mouth and eyes that didn't miss a thing. Aware of his background, she had to concede a compelling ruthlessness lurked beneath the surface of his control.

'Good morning.' He included Tony in the greeting. 'I trust you both slept well?'

Ariane met his gaze with level coolness. 'Thank you.' Nerves were something she'd learnt to disguise, and it irked her that this man unsettled her more than most.

Recognition of sexual chemistry, that's all it is, she rationalised, and did her best to dismiss it.

She was here to do a job. What was more, she had no interest in men. Especially someone of Manolo del Guardo's calibre.

'Tony is about through checking the sound equipment.' Professionalism was everything. 'Is there anything in the questionnaire you'd like to discuss at this point?'

One eyebrow rose. 'I'm familiar with the interview process.'

'Yes, of course.' A conciliatory smile offered a soothing salve. 'As you're aware, we intend to focus on three key elements: your background; business success; your nominated charity interest. With sufficient personal details to give the interview an individual touch and tie it all together.'

Doing that would be a challenge. Perhaps more than she bargained for. This man was no pushover, and far too warily astute to be led into any indiscriminate revelations.

She'd suggested 'smart casual wear' for the morning session. Trousers by Armani, shirt by Versace. She was willing to swear both styles had been worn by male models in a fashion show she'd *compèred* recently.

A deliberate choice on Manolo del Guardo's part?

'Perhaps we could make a start?'

Ariane studied his features with analytical appraisal, and steadfastly ignored the tension coiling inside her stomach as he held her gaze.

'Something bothers you?'

You do. In spades. 'I'd like to apply a light make-up.' She turned towards a small cosmetic box she always carried for just this purpose. 'Just the merest touch.'

'No.'

The drawling voice held a silky softness that caused her to momentarily freeze before swinging back to face him. 'We're talking a faint coverage of translucent powder, nothing more.'

'No.'

It wasn't much after nine in the morning, and they'd already encountered a hiccup. She sought to appease. 'It's standard procedure.'

'But not one I choose to observe.'

OK, so make-up was a no-go. She could handle that.

'Would you care to take a seat?' It wasn't so much a suggestion as a directive, and it earned her a contemplative look.

'And if I prefer to stand?'

He was toying with her. 'Mr del Guardo—'

'I thought we agreed on informality?'

This was going to be one hell of a weekend. 'Manolo,' she conceded, and he inclined his head.

'Gracias.'

'Let's get you wired.' Tony moved forward with two remote microphones, handed one to Ariane and fixed the other to the V of Manolo del Guardo's shirt.

The ball is in *your* court, you're in charge, you have control.

Sure, Ariane conceded with silent cynicism. And cows jump over the moon!

Dealing with an ego was part of the job, and she'd dealt with a few in her time. 'I'd like to keep this as relaxed and informal as possible.' She deliberately held his gaze. 'Visual and audio will be edited, and you'll have control over final content.'

His eyes held a dark intensity that could sear the soul. Could they also soothe?

Oh, hell, where had *that* come from?

'I'll remind you, any attempt at clever journalistic tactics on your part will be met with silence.'

Oh, my. Ariane drew herself up to her full height and took a slow, steady breath. 'Point taken.' She even managed a faint smile. 'Shall we begin?'

An hour later she had nothing more on Manolo del Guardo than what was already available in previous Press releases. Which meant she had to work a little harder.

'Tell me what it was like growing up in the 'hood.'

The faint smile didn't reach his eyes. 'You want I should draw a picture?' Street gangs, poverty, where survival meant being one step ahead of the law in alleyways where one false move could bring a knife in the ribs…or worse?

'I imagine it was tough.'

He doubted her imagination stretched as far as the reality. Except he'd managed to get out and move on. Lean years when he'd worked his butt off twenty by seven, taking risks only the brave or a fool would touch.

'The prime motivation was to survive.'

His voice held an edge of mockery, and a wealth of *living* lurked in the depths of those dark eyes. Elements she could only guess at.

'Perhaps you'd care to elaborate?'

'I don't see the need to provide a vicarious insight into the days of my youth.'

OK, so he was going to play hardball. 'Self-protection, or a need to bury your past?'

He didn't move, yet she had the sensation his powerful body suddenly went on full alert.

The silence in the room became a palpable entity, and she held her breath, waiting for a display of temperament.

It didn't happen, and there was little she could detect beneath his obsidian gaze.

Supreme control, she registered, and wondered what it would take to break it. A faint shivery sensation threatened to slither the length of her spine at the thought of what direction his anger might take...certain in her mind it would be laser-swift and deadly.

Ariane's attention was so focused on the man that at first she didn't register the faint sound of a baby's cry.

'You'll have to excuse me.' Manolo rose to his feet in one fluid movement and crossed to the door.

It was then she heard the angry wail of a distressed babe, a sound that rose to a crescendo in seconds.

Ariane signalled for Tony to cut, and followed Manolo del Guardo into the foyer.

The sight of him cradling a baby in the curve of his arm caused the breath to catch in her throat.

At that moment he turned, and she stood locked into immobility at the ruthless intensity of his gaze. 'Your intrusion is not welcome.' His voice was dangerously soft, and the infant's wailing increased.

She had the unbearable urge to take the child and attempt to soothe its pain. 'The camera isn't on, nor is the sound.'

The fate of Manolo del Guardo's late wife was common knowledge; so too was the existence of their daughter. Except no photos of the child had reached the media.

'Ensure it remains that way.'

The infant's wailing intensified, then subsided into a series of cross, hiccuping cries.

Ariane couldn't help herself. 'She has colic.'

'And you know this...because?'

She wanted to hit him. Instead she held her breath and counted to three before releasing it. She even managed a negligible shrug. 'We can take up where we left off when you've settled your daughter into the nanny's care.'

'Difficult, when the girl walked out yesterday, and a replacement isn't due until mid-week.'

'I'm sorry.'

Was that genuine concern? Or a polite act? Manolo opted for the latter. 'We'll reconvene after lunch.' He glanced at his watch. 'At two.'

He headed towards the stairs, and Ariane retraced her steps to find Tony running a review of the morning's taping.

'We're taking a break?'

'Dismissed until two.' She crossed to where he stood. 'What do you think?'

'So far so good. He's ice.'

'And won't crack?'

He shot her a direct look as the tape went into rewind. 'Waste of time to even try.'

Ariane viewed the morning's session with an analytical eye, then retrieved her notebook, made a few notations and returned it to her briefcase.

There was half an hour until lunch, and she felt the pressing need for some fresh air. 'I'm going to take a walk in the grounds.'

'And examine the plant life?'

'You have a better suggestion?'

Tony offered a wicked smile. 'You could go pound the punching bag in the gym.'

'Talk to me at day's end. Although kickboxing is more my style. You could join me.'

'Sorry, sweetheart. I'm not into masochism.'

She wrinkled her nose at him. 'I might let you win.'

He lifted both hands in mock-capitulation. 'Do me a favour, and go smell the roses.'

'While you do…what?'

His slow grin held a teasing quality. 'Kick back and anticipate this afternoon's verbal interaction.'

Ariane rolled her eyes. 'How come you get to have all the fun?'

He waited a beat, then offered quietly, 'Watch out for yourself.'

A friend, as well as an associate, he saw too much. 'Always.'

The automatic assurance didn't fool either of them, and Ariane collected her cellphone before making her way to the rear of the house.

French doors led onto a large terrace, and she crossed it, then descended a set of stone steps to a paved courtyard.

The grounds were larger than she'd expected, with an expanse of immaculate lawn. Garden beds abounded with an array of flora in bloom, a riot of colour and green foliage, exquisite topiary. There was a gazebo, painted white with a peaked roof and decorative scrolls. A water fountain stood nearby, and she sighted a marble birdbath.

Shrubbery, garden seats—it was close to picture perfect, and she wondered if Manolo del Guardo surrounded himself with beautiful objects because he genuinely enjoyed them, or whether they were merely the possessions expected of a wealthy man. Suggested, supplied and maintained to create an image.

The house…mansion, she corrected mentally. Had he employed a team of interior decorators and given them carte blanche?

Her cellphone beeped and promptly went to message-bank, providing a reminder she should check the morning's incoming calls.

Three, she determined a few minutes later, two of which were from Roger. A sick feeling twisted her stomach at the brief, crude words.

Ignore him, she counselled silently, hating the wiliness of his psychosis. He rarely rang from the same number twice, switching SIM cards, using numerous pay-phones in a game devised to fool her so she'd engage each call or message. Even in the few seconds it took to hit the *erase* button, he managed to achieve his objective.

Roger was the reason she'd taken up martial arts. For the discipline and control…as a form of protection and a means of channelling her anger against his intrusive harassment.

Ariane pocketed the cellphone and deliberately focused her attention on her surroundings. It was a beautiful summer's day, with only a few drifts of cloud in the sky. The warmth of the sun caressed her skin, and the air held the sweetness of flowers in bloom, their colours, some muted, many bright, a visual delight.

A short while later she returned indoors, freshened up, then she joined Tony in the dining room for lunch. Thin slices of veal, Parma ham, salads and fresh bread, followed by a delectable fruit salad.

There was time to retouch her make-up and smooth her hair before joining Tony in the designated interview room, where she went over her notes and the questions she wanted to pose during the afternoon taping.

Manolo del Guardo appeared shortly after two, in, unless she was mistaken, a change of shirt. White, top few buttons undone, with cuffs rolled back, the difference in style was minimal, and probably unnoticeable to the untrained eye.

She attempted to qualify it as an integral part of the job, and knew she lied. Everything about this man caught and held her interest.

The animalistic sense of power combined with a dramatic mesh of elemental ruthlessness and latent sensuality. Add leashed savagery, and it became a lethal mix.

Be professional, *think* interview quality, and ignore the exigent magnetism, Ariane advised silently. A derisive laugh rose and died in her throat. Sure, as if that was likely to happen.

'This afternoon I'd like to concentrate on your entry into the business arena,' she began. 'A few early breaks, your motivation to succeed, risks.' She met his gaze and held it. 'Highlights charting your career.'

Manolo took in her slender frame, ash-blonde hair in its sleek style, hazel green-flecked eyes, the small but determined chin, her lush mouth.

Had anyone told her those eyes became dark green when she was angry? An emotion she hid well, and one he found intriguing.

She'd done her research, he conceded as he answered her questions and offered information already known to the media.

'No dabbling in illegals in a quest to build your empire?'

For years he'd walked on the right side of the law, but there were some deals done in his early teens of which he was not particularly proud.

'Perhaps you'd care to define ''illegals''?'

His drawling tone was silk-smooth and dangerous beneath the dispassionate imperturbability.

'Does it need defining?'

'The implication covers a broad spectrum.'

'Could one assume your evasion of the question supplies its own answer?'

'Are you levelling an accusation?'

Oh, lord, he could have a team of top-flight lawyers breathing down her neck in an instant. 'No.' Her tone was steady, and she effected a polite smile. 'Merely voicing admiration for the extent of your wealth in relation to the time in which you've achieved it.'

'I'll accept that as a compliment.'

He wanted to strangle her. She could sense it beneath the surface of his control.

A few more questions and she was done for the afternoon. She watched as Manolo del Guardo rose from his chair, inclined his head and walked from the room.

'He let you get away unscathed.'

Tony's comment should have brought her some satisfaction. Instead she could only wonder at the ease with which Manolo del Guardo had allowed her to dance so close to the line between the provocative and the sensational.

'Yes.' She gathered paperwork and slid it into her briefcase.

'It's a shame we can't wrap it up tonight.'

Ariane slung the leather strap over one shoulder. 'I understand our host has a pressing engagement for the evening.'

Tony placed the camera in its case and locked it. 'We could go grab a pizza, take in a movie.'

'Count me out.' She moved towards the door. 'I'm going to try out the lap pool, have dinner here, then catch an early night.'

'Maybe that's not such a bad idea. We were given permission to avail ourselves of the entertainment room. Maybe Santos will let us microwave popcorn?'

'In your dreams.' She offered him a musing grin. 'Does this look like a home that has popcorn in the pantry?'

With that parting salvo she crossed the foyer and ascended the stairs, choosing to check her cellphone messages as she made her way to her room.

Roger…again. Twice, she determined, and stifled a pithy oath. Would the man ever cease with his harassment? Catching his first few words before she hit *erase* was almost as bad as listening to the entire message, for the damage was done. He'd succeeded in reaching her, and in his book that was enough.

Let it go. They were only words. Take a deep breath.

Ariane repeated the silent mantra as she slipped out of her clothes and donned the swimsuit she'd tossed into her bag on the off-chance she might use it. Then she pulled on jogging-bottoms and top, caught up a towel and made her way down to the lower level.

The gym was impressive, the equipment expensive, and she crossed to the indoor lap pool, slid into the water and began a punishing series of laps, back and forth until she could feel the pull of muscles.

It felt good to expend pent-up energy, and she emerged, crossed to the shower, then donned sweats and returned to her room to change for dinner.

After a pleasant meal, they took coffee into the entertainment room and watched a movie on DVD.

When it finished Ariane rose to her feet. 'Goodnight.'

Tony slotted in another movie, then sank back into a comfortable chair. 'See you at breakfast.'

CHAPTER THREE

ARIANE was unsure what woke her. Only that something had, and she lay still, listening to the silence, wondering if she'd slipped into consciousness from a dream.

Then she heard it, the distant cry of a fractious babe. Manolo del Guardo's daughter. Awake and, from the sound of it, in pain.

What time was it? She checked her watch…almost midnight. Any second now Manolo or, if he hadn't returned home, Santos would tend to Christina.

The cries continued, and Ariane didn't pause for thought as she slid out of bed, snagged her robe and shrugged into it, then made her way along the gallery.

Electric wall sconces turned low provided a dim light, and she moved quickly past a few closed doors, then paused outside the room where the sound seemed the loudest. A slight qualm caused a momentary hesitation, then at a further wail she discarded it and opened the door.

Ariane barely registered the room with its soft lighting as she crossed to the cot. Her attention was focused on the distressed babe.

'Poor little *petite*, hmm?' She scooped the child up

and held her against one shoulder, instinctively sooth-ing the small back. 'Let's guess, shall we? You're hungry? Wet? In pain?' She touched her cheek to the small head. 'Or all three?'

At almost six months of age, was she still having a late-night bottle? There had to be a feeding schedule around somewhere. But not in plain sight, she regis-tered.

'OK, little one, let's do a nappy change and see if that helps any.'

Ariane heard a sound and turned towards the door to discover Santos framed in the aperture. 'I heard her crying via the monitor, and came as quickly as I could.'

She laid the babe on the bed nestled against one wall and deftly effected a nappy change, speaking softly as she did so. 'There we go, angel. Now, if only you could talk, we'd know if it's a tooth ready to come through, or a tummy pain.'

'I'll take over.'

She spared Santos a measured look. 'Because you feel you should, or you doubt my ability to cope?'

'On the contrary. You seem to be doing just fine. Christina has stopped crying.'

A very satisfactory burp issued forth, and Ariane smiled. 'Any more, sweetheart?' Almost on command there was another. 'Does she usually have a bottle? I couldn't see a feeding schedule.' She stroked a sooth-ing finger over the babe's cheek.

'Probably because the last nanny didn't keep one,' Santos offered drily.

Obviously nannies, plural, were a sensitive subject.

'I gave Christina a bottle at eight, and she has, I understand, been sleeping through until around five in the morning.'

But not tonight. Poor wee mite. No mother to cuddle her, a father who left her in the care of professionals and was too busy adding millions to his incredible fortune…

'Problems, Santos?'

Think of the devil, and he appeared.

'Christina is finding it difficult to settle.'

Manolo shrugged out of his dinner jacket and tossed it over a chair, then he loosened his tie and turned back the cuffs of his shirt.

Even to Ariane's jaded eye he was too ruggedly attractive for his own good. The height, breadth of shoulder, his stance, and compelling facial features.

'My apologies. I was unexpectedly delayed.'

Was it her imagination, or did she catch a telling glance pass between Manolo del Guardo and Santos?

'Ariane heard Christina's cry and reached her ahead of me.' The explanation came from Santos, and Manolo inclined his head in her direction.

'Thank you for your concern.'

But you can go now? The implication was apparent. It was totally weird, but she wanted to delay the inevitable a little longer. Holding the babe felt so…good. Almost in silent unison the babe nuzzled a little, and Ariane eased the knuckle of her little finger close to the babe's mouth. Almost at once the babe began suckling as Ariane continued to stroke the tiny cheek.

Manolo's gaze narrowed fractionally. 'I'll take Christina.' He checked his watch. 'I guess it won't hurt to give her another bottle.'

'She might settle back to sleep without one.' She could hardly hold the babe any longer, and she gently eased her towards her father.

Christina's protest was immediate, and voluble.

Ariane's heart turned over at the sound, and she resisted the impulse to reach out and soothe the babe.

'It would appear you have a certain empathy with the young.'

A compliment? Should she admit to having had some practice? 'I reported the effects of war on children during the conflict in Kosovo.'

Very few were aware her experience was hands-on, that she'd spent time in severely understaffed hospital wards, helping out, or that she'd chosen to stay until trained staff arrived on the scene.

'Where chaos reigned and depleted medical supplies were the norm.' Manolo subjected her to a steady appraisal.

A calculated guess, based on media releases at the time?

'You were given the opportunity to fly out with

departing media staff, yet you refused,' he continued. 'Instead you ate rationed food, opted to sleep on a mattress on the floor of an infirmary and tended the sick twenty-four seven.'

He couldn't know that, unless—

'No one enters my home without undergoing a full investigation,' he informed quietly.

No one?

'No.'

Oh, hell, that was just what she needed…someone who could read her mind.

Christina uttered a cry in protest, then settled into full voice with renewed fervour.

Ariane's hands itched to take back the babe, heat a feeding bottle and cradle her close. Yet she didn't have the right.

'Goodnight.' Her voice came out sounding stiff and incredibly polite.

'Thank you.' There was no cynicism apparent, and she turned as she reached the door.

'No problem.'

It was Ariane's suggestion stage three of the interview be taped in Manolo del Guardo's study…or library, office…whatever he chose to call the room where most of the business action took place away from his corporate offices.

For this occasion she'd requested formal attire, and he didn't disappoint.

An impeccably tailored suit, blue cotton shirt and matching silk tie conveyed the outer trappings of a very successful businessman.

'I imagine it won't take long to set up your equipment?'

'I can do that while Ariane gives you a run-through,' Tony assured.

Ariane was tempted to ask if Christina was OK, whether she'd slept well…and barely managed to pull herself up as she followed Manolo through the foyer to a spacious room lined with floor-to-ceiling bookcases.

There was a large executive desk, comfortable leather buttoned chairs, the usual fax, computer, printer.

She checked her clipboard, then studied the room. The natural light seemed fine. 'I think we'll begin with you seated behind the desk. After a few questions you can stand, perhaps cross to the bookcases.' She glanced towards Tony. 'You could do a slow pan with the camera.' He gave a nod in silent agreement. 'Then we can conclude with Manolo seated in one of those chairs.'

In a few hours they'd be able to wrap it. Then they could pack up and leave. Another job done. Well, there was the grunt work of editing and mixing. Tony already had a sweeping external shot of the tall, modern, downtown building housing the Del Guardo

Corporation, together with a small footage of the luxurious entry foyer.

As per detailed instructions, there would be no external shots of his private home or an indication of its location. No outward display of his cars, the cruiser he was purported to own, or the private jet.

Manolo del Guardo could easily have become an 'if you've got it, flaunt it' type of tycoon. Instead, he guarded his home and daughter with the type of hi-tech electronic privacy reserved for royalty and the Hollywood glitterati.

'This morning we'll focus on your charity interest, how and why you founded the organisation, your contributions, achievements and goals.'

Ariane knew most of it, for she'd carefully researched all the information available. Professionally, the media interest was in the man, his background and his success. The charity, while laudable, was a side issue.

Yet there could be no doubt Manolo del Guardo's passion was genuine, and she found herself taking more time than she'd intended.

It was common knowledge the Del Guardo Corporation made amenities available for street kids, with a gym, dojo, safe-houses where they could sleep and get a meal. There were professional counsellors on hand, together with former street kids who ran straight and knew first-hand what it was like to live on the streets, what it took to break clear from gangs who ruled by fear.

'Your personal contribution must be quite substantial. Would you care to indicate a ballpark figure?'

'No.'

'Are we talking millions?' Ariane persisted, and heard his drawled response,

'I believe I've already answered the question.'

'Do you actively participate?'

His level gaze was vaguely unsettling. 'I make a point of it,' he allowed quietly.

She gave Tony a prearranged signal, and concluded the interview. It was after midday, almost one, and she really wanted out of here.

The man's sexual chemistry disturbed and unsettled her. She didn't want it, didn't like it…and found it impossible to ignore.

'We'll run a contact telephone number for the charity foundation's arm of your corporation, and it will remain on-screen as the credits roll.'

Manolo uncurled his lengthy frame from the chair. 'Thank you. I'd like to view the morning's taping.' He moved towards the door, opened it, and stood to one side.

'Tony will run it through for you.'

That would give her time to check any messages, and transfer her bag downstairs.

'Ariane.' She paused as she drew level with him,

and she tilted her head to meet his gaze. This close she was all too aware of his height and breadth of shoulder. The clean smell of freshly laundered clothes mingled with a hint of cologne, and she suddenly had difficulty regulating her breathing.

'There's something I'd like to discuss with you.'

Oh, dammit, he was going to take her to task over some of her questions, suggest a stringent editing she wouldn't agree to, and they'd resort to a clash of verbal swords.

'Here?'

Tony was dismantling equipment with the ease of long practice.

'You're not comfortable with *here*?'

I'm not comfortable with *you*, she offered silently. Get over it!

Tony moved towards the door, and only she glimpsed his expressive eye-roll as he passed from the room.

Attack was often the best form of defence. 'You have a complaint?'

'On the contrary. A request.'

No complaint was good. The knot in her stomach eased a little. 'And that would be?'

'I understand you're due for a break following this assignment.'

Was there anything he didn't know? Don't answer that!

All Manolo del Guardo had to do was make a few phone calls...or have someone do it for him.

'Yes.' She planned taking in a few movies, indulging in some serious retail therapy, and catching up with friends. Curious, she queried, 'Perhaps you'd care to explain where this is leading?'

'Would you be prepared to stay on for a few days to care for Christina until the agency can supply another nanny?'

Her breath hitched, then steadied as she deliberately stifled her sense of incredulity. 'This is a joke, right?'

'It's a serious offer.' He named a figure that sent her eyebrows lifting high.

'I don't have any nanny qualifications.'

'You've been able to bond with my daughter.'

She regarded him carefully. 'Christina responded to warmth and affection. I doubt it's anything personal.'

'She responded to *you*,' he reiterated firmly. 'Therefore the very reason for my request.'

'You hardly know me.'

His faint smile was a mere facsimile. 'On the contrary.' It wasn't difficult to relay a collection of facts. Her age, place of birth, her places of employment, where she lived. 'Your father is contracted to an oil company whose offices are dotted throughout the Middle East, and you see your parents each year. You have a brother, Alex, two years your senior, who holds a high-powered engineering position and is based in Hong Kong. You were married, briefly,' he continued, watching those beautiful eyes become stormy. 'Went through a difficult divorce, and now have a restraining order against your ex-husband for harassment. You don't have a current partner, rarely date…' His gaze held hers. 'Shall I go on?'

She closed her eyes briefly to mask the anger threatening her control, then opened them again. 'Such investigation amounts to an invasion of my privacy.'

'Correction,' Manolo declared drily. 'I consider it essential protection.'

'Yours,' she accorded stiffly.

'That of my daughter,' he amended. 'And anyone who shares my home, however briefly.'

'Next, you'll relay Santos' position as chef and general factotum is secondary to being bodyguard?' It was more statement than query, and Manolo's silence provided an answer.

A baby's cry sounded close by, followed by another, and they both turned as Santos entered the room with Christina nestled against one shoulder and a bottle of formula held in his hand.

Circumstance, or conspiracy? Whatever, Ariane's heart melted at the sight of the babe's reddened face, the small fist clutched against her mouth.

Manolo transferred his daughter, collected the bottle and settled into a chair, whereby Christina latched onto the teat and suckled far too fast.

Ariane made an involuntary move towards the babe, then stopped herself. 'She's drinking too quickly.' No wonder the poor little mite was restless. She probably suffered from stomachache.

'You have any suggestions to offer?'

'She needs a different teat, one that'll slow her down a little.'

'I'll visit the nearest pharmacy and purchase a selection,' Santos said at once and retreated into the hallway to go do that very thing.

The phone on his desk rang, and Ariane silently gestured to take over feeding Christina while he took the call.

Dear heaven, she was such a sweet little thing. She had her father's dark hair, and her skin was as soft as a rose petal.

Ariane tuned out Manolo's voice and focused on the babe, easing the teat to minimise the gulp-like feeding.

All too soon the bottle was empty, and Ariane took care of the burping process, aware as she did so that Manolo had finished his call.

The silence seemed a tangible entity, and one he broke minutes later.

'What will it take?' He added a sizable bonus to the figure previously offered.

She met and held his gaze. 'Don't insult me by making money an issue.'

He leaned one hip against the edge of the desk. 'When is money not an issue?' His voice was a cynical drawl, the New York accent pronounced as he studied the young woman competently tending his child.

Was her apparent integrity real, or simply an act? And why should he care? Christina's welfare was his prime concern. Dammit, he was due to fly to Melbourne in the morning for an important meeting. At worst, he could arrange to put his daughter into daycare nursery for the day and take the late-afternoon flight home. But the babe had been restless and distressed almost from birth, and factoring in a series of nannies... He was loath to remove Christina from her immediate environment. The alternative was to have Santos and Maria, the daily house-cleaner, juggle his daughter's care.

'Please.' It was a last-ditch effort.

That was all it took, a single word. Yet Ariane wasn't prepared to let him off the hook too easily. It didn't escape her that having Santos bring the babe into the study was not merely coincidental.

'You don't play fair.'

He played to win. Whatever it took, by whatever means at his disposal. 'Would it be such a hardship?'

More than you know. Yet there was only one answer she could give with the babe cradled close against her shoulder, the sweet, clean baby smell teasing her nostrils.

It's only for a few days, she assured silently. 'I'll stay.'

'Thank you.' Manolo straightened away from the desk. 'Santos will organise a late lunch. That will give you time to settle Christina for her afternoon nap.'

She also needed to inform Tony she wouldn't be leaving with him, and why. His reaction was a given, and didn't disappoint.

'So he got to you, huh?'

Tony had been part of the team during the Kosovo debacle. He hadn't approved of her staying on then, any more than he did now.

He trailed light fingers down her cheek. 'St Ariane, protector of the young.' He pressed a finger to her lips. 'Take care.'

'Always.'

His smile held genuine warmth. 'OK, I'm out of here. Catch up soon?'

'Count on it.'

CHAPTER FOUR

LUNCH was a pleasant meal eaten solo on the terrace. The view out over the harbour was magnificent, with the sparkling blue waters busy with numerous craft. She counted a hydrofoil, a tug leading a tanker in to port, a departing cruise liner.

The city-scape, with its tall buildings, bright flashing neon signs, provided a multidimensional backdrop for the harbour bridge, the distinctive architecture of the opera house.

Wherever she travelled, Sydney was *home*. There was an apartment in trendy Double Bay, a late-model BMW, and she enjoyed an interesting life. With one exception. Roger.

Given she was now officially on her own time, she could dispense with her pager and turn off her cellphone.

Changing her number was a fruitless exercise. She'd been there, done that so many times, and all it achieved was a twenty-four-hour break before her ex-husband managed to crack the telephone company's privacy code and access her new number.

Instead, she took the advice of legal counsel and

recorded Roger's messages at day's end. His letters were retained, unopened, for legal reference.

A faint cry echoed from the baby monitor attached to her jeans, and she gave the sound her full attention. It was too soon for Christina's next feed, and she listened to the snuffling, the increasing protest that rapidly developed into a continuous wail as she entered the nursery.

A warm bath, some splashing fun, a few cuddles would help fill the time. It would also assist the bonding process…but not too much, Ariane warned silently, for her time as carer would be very short.

It was there Manolo found them, woman and child, taking such delight in each other he stood silently observing the scene for several long seconds before making his presence known.

'Any problems?'

Ariane turned slowly towards the man leaning indolently at ease against the door-frame. 'No. It's almost time for Christina's dinner.' Puréed vegetables, which she'd organised with Santos.

'Is there anything you need from your apartment? If so, Santos will drive you there.' He straightened and moved into the room. 'You might want to collect your car.'

A few changes of clothes were a definite. 'Thanks. I'll feed and settle Christina first. Shall we say an hour from now?'

'I'll inform Santos.'

It was almost six when she rode the lift to her apartment. The first thing she did was turn on the air-conditioning to circulate some air and cool the interior down, then she checked her answering-machine and dealt with the tension curling in her stomach at the flashing numerical dial. Ten messages recorded, most if not all were probably generated by Roger.

Pack first, riffle through the mail she'd collected at Reception, run the answering-machine, then leave… that was the plan.

It should have worked, and almost did. The recorded messages were repetitive, sickening, and as much as she endeavoured to dismiss the sound of Roger's voice, it lingered intrusively as she took the lift down to the underground car park.

If she could hit him, she would! Except that wasn't a viable option. At least it wasn't a wise one.

As if wisdom had anything to do with it, she reflected as she crossed towards her designated parking bay.

Something caught her eye, and she paused, frowning. What the…?

A flat front tyre. Oh, *great*. Just what she needed.

Well, it wouldn't be the first time she'd had to change a tyre, she resolved as she unlocked the car and threw her bag onto the back seat before crossing to the boot.

As to how long it would take…who was counting?

The change-over completed, she slid in behind the

wheel, fired the engine and began reversing…only to feel the soft clunking sound of metal rim on concrete.

Two flat tyres? Hell, surely not? Fate couldn't be so unkind.

Close examination proved that both front tyres had been slashed.

Roger? Who else would do something like this?

Ariane collected her bag, locked the car, and took the lift to Reception, where she notified the apartment-building manager, the police, then rang for a cab to take her to Manolo del Guardo's Point Piper mansion.

At the main gates she paid the driver, cleared security through the audio-visual monitor, and accessed the driveway.

Santos met her at the front door, and took the bag from her hand. 'You don't have your car?'

Ariane effected a wry smile as she entered the lobby. 'Unfortunately not. Someone chose to slash two of my tyres.'

The man's eyes narrowed. 'I imagine you've notified the authorities?'

'Taken care of. Is Christina OK?'

'Manolo gave her a bottle and settled her. She's asleep.' He indicated the bag. 'I'll take this to your room.'

'Oh, please.' She reached for it. 'It's not heavy.'

Santos retained it in a firm grasp. 'Dinner will be ready in thirty minutes.'

Discretion was the key. Besides, she didn't feel like instigating a verbal tussle over something as minor as who got to take her bag upstairs.

There was time to check on Christina before returning to her room to change her jeans for a straight black skirt, fitted white blouse, then she slid her feet into medium-heeled pumps.

Fixing her hair into a casual knot atop her head, she touched colour to her lips, pocketed the remote baby monitor, then she made her way downstairs.

It came as something of a surprise to discover the dining table held a few covered dishes and two place-settings. Santos was eating with her?

'Please. Take a seat.'

Ariane turned at the sound of Manolo's drawling voice. The man had the lithe grace of a large cat. Silent and deadly.

He'd exchanged the formal suit he'd worn during the morning's interview for black tailored trousers and a chambray shirt which emphasised his breadth of shoulder, trim waist and lean hips.

There was little about Manolo del Guardo that hinted at his background. Any rough edges had been smoothed out long ago as he'd steadily acquired the layers of wealth and respectability.

Yet instinct warned a primitive ruthlessness existed on some deep, intrinsic level. An emotion, unleashed, hinted at deadly power.

It was a quality that fascinated and frightened, she

perceived, depending which side of the fence you were on.

'We both need to eat,' Manolo ventured. 'Why not have the meal together?'

Why not, indeed? Except she wasn't a guest, nor was she an employee. Substitute nanny? Somehow *friend* didn't quite fit.

Manolo del Guardo wasn't the most comfortable man to be around. From her own perspective, she added, all too aware of the effect he had on her composure. Attempting to rationalise *why* failed to provide an answer.

Even during her brief courtship with Roger, when she was convinced marriage to him would be a dream come true, she hadn't felt the blood fizz in her veins.

A hollow laugh rose and died in her throat. Forget *fizz*…lightning bolt was more accurate. All her senses went on to full-alert mode whenever she was in Manolo del Guardo's presence.

Crazy. And to think she'd willingly agreed to remain in his home and take care of his child…it bordered on insanity. She should have declined his offer and run as fast as possible back to her safe life.

'Can I get you a drink?'

Oh, for heaven's sake, get a grip! 'Something long, cool and non-alcoholic.'

He filled a glass with mineral water, added lemon, poured himself some wine and placed both within easy reach.

'Inform Santos which firm is supplying and fitting the tyres, and he'll arrange to have your car brought here.'

It was impossible news of her misadventure hadn't reached his ears. It would be more than Santos' job was worth not to inform Manolo del Guardo of every little thing affecting his household and those who occupied it.

'That isn't necessary.'

Manolo removed the covers to reveal a dish of steaming paella, an accompanying salad, and warm bread rolls. With ease he collected her plate and served her a portion before helping himself.

'Why have the car returned to your apartment building where it'll continue to be at risk?'

'All I'll gain is a few days. It's possible Roger may not have been involved.' Who was she trying to fool? 'The episode will inevitably be dismissed as a random act of vandalism.'

'If he's having you watched,' Manolo offered steadily, 'he'll be aware Tony drove away from here alone.'

'Do you think that hasn't already occurred to me?'

He speared a delectable prawn and ate it, then paused to sample the wine. 'What connotation is he likely to put on you remaining here with me?'

She flashed him a direct look. 'I'm not *with* you.'

'He doesn't know that.'

'The size of your ego is staggering.'

'While your honesty is refreshing.' His voice was pure silk, the drawling accent pronounced. 'But in this case, misplaced. I was referring to your ex-husband's jealousy and whether it has the potential to lead to violence.'

The nerves in her stomach tightened into a painful ball. 'If you'd prefer me to leave, please say so.'

One eyebrow slanted. 'Why would I ask you to leave?'

'I'm a security risk.'

'My home and grounds are under constant surveillance with state-of-the-art technology,' he reminded as he reached for the salad. 'You are more safe beneath my roof than anywhere else.'

'How reassuring.'

'Cynicism doesn't suit you.'

Ariane pushed her plate to one side, her appetite gone. She rose to her feet. 'If you'll excuse me, I'll go check Christina.'

'Sit down.'

She looked at him in silent askance.

'My daughter's slightest sound is audible via the monitor.' He indicated the seat she'd just vacated.

'Eat.'

Who did he think he was? Don't answer that, an imp admonished silently. 'Is that an order?'

He replaced his fork and leaned back in his chair to regard her with a compelling scrutiny she found distinctly unnerving. 'A suggestion.'

Ariane remained on her feet. 'In that case—'

'Sit down...please. I'm taking the early-morning flight to Melbourne tomorrow on business, and won't return until late.' He regarded her steadily. 'Santos can reach me at any time should the need arise.'

She remained standing. 'I'm sure Christina will be fine.'

'Yes.' He had every confidence his daughter would be in good hands. Ariane Celeste, however, wasn't fine, and he had to wonder why that should bother him.

He hadn't experienced quite this degree of physical attraction to a woman in a while, despite the many who deliberately set out to tempt him.

Love, the true 'until death us do part' kind, didn't form part of his vocabulary, and he held doubt it existed outside the pages of fiction.

A snuffling sound came through the baby monitor, followed by a single cry that rapidly developed into a full crescendo.

'I'll see to Christina.' She even managed a polite smile as she took refuge in the excuse to escape.

Manolo twirled the crystal wine goblet and surveyed its contents with contemplative uninterest, before replacing it on the table, his appetite for the food and wine gone.

There were graphs he needed to study, adjust and print out ready for tomorrow's meeting. He also wanted to amend his notes.

'You're done?'

He turned towards Santos, and inclined his head.

'Valentina Vaquez rang and left a message for you to call.'

Manolo stifled a wry grimace. This had to be Valentina's third call today. The woman was nothing if not persistent. What excuse would she give this time as the reason for her call? An invitation to some event she felt he shouldn't miss?

He rose to his feet and crossed to the coffee-maker, where he poured steaming black liquid into a cup. 'I'll take this into the office.'

It was late when he closed his laptop and made his way upstairs. He reached the upper level and turned towards his suite at the end of the hallway.

The door to the nursery was slightly ajar, and he was about to check when he heard a soft feminine voice crooning a familiar lullaby.

Manolo waited a beat, then slowly pushed the door open. Christina was on the verge of sleep with her cheek tucked in against the curve of Ariane's neck.

It was an image he'd witnessed before in the five and a half months since Christina's birth with a series of live-in nannies. Professional childminders, but none had looked more in tune with caring for a young child than the woman who now held his daughter.

At that moment Ariane turned, caught sight of him, and she lifted a finger to her lips, then she crossed to the cot and gently lowered the child down.

Christina didn't stir, and Ariane stood quietly for a few minutes before motioning her intention to leave the room.

The illumination from the wall sconces cast a soft light, and she felt her heart rate pick up to a throbbing beat at his close proximity.

There was little she could do to control the sudden onset of nervous tension, or the almost breathless sensation that made her supremely conscious of every breath she took.

She didn't like the feeling, didn't like *him*... although that wasn't strictly true. It wasn't so much the man, but the degree of sexual chemistry he managed to exude. Worse...her reaction to it.

With a murmured 'goodnight' she returned to her room. It was late, she should get some sleep. Instead she lay awake, staring at the darkened ceiling for what seemed an age, her mind too active with Roger's hateful messages, the likelihood he'd stepped up his stalking campaign, and last but not least...why she'd agreed to stay on in Manolo del Guardo's home when every sane cell in her body urged her to flee as far away from him as fast as she could.

Except Christina's image filled her mind, and she plumped her pillow in restrained frustration. How could she leave? If she did, her conscience would haunt her for years to come.

Maybe a miracle would occur and the agency

would ring tomorrow with a replacement nanny who was prepared to make an immediate start.

Maybe she should pray.

The only problem being it had been a while since the deity appeared to be on her wavelength!

Ariane woke early, tended to Christina, then, showered and dressed, she went downstairs, collected the day's newspaper and ate breakfast on the terrace.

Of Manolo there was no sign, and she could only surmise he'd already left for the airport.

She told herself she was relieved as she devoted the day to his daughter. There was satisfaction in the child's response, the tentative smiles, an occasional giggle when teased, and there was both pleasure and pain in Christina's response.

A pleasantly plump woman in her early forties occupied the kitchen when Ariane went down to prepare Christina's custard and apple for lunch.

Santos performed the introduction, adding Maria came in each day to clean and tend to the laundry.

'I have five children,' Maria informed cheerfully.

Italian, Spanish? It was difficult to detect which, and Ariane offered a smile in response. 'They must keep you busy.'

'Very busy.' Maria chuckled. 'We laugh, we fight. We eat. It is a good life.'

And work hard, Ariane deduced.

'I've prepared a chicken salad with fruit to follow,'

Santos informed. 'Unless you'd prefer something else?'

'Chicken salad sounds great.'

Maria glanced up from wiping down the cupboards. 'Christina, she is teething, yes? Poor little one. Nannies are not the same as a mother.'

Ariane was inclined to agree. So why did the thought bother her more than it should?

It was something she endeavoured to dismiss as she returned to the nursery with Christina's lunch.

Toys were in abundance, children's books, colourful hanging mobiles, prints occupying space on the walls. Everything a child could possibly need, and more.

There had to be a pram somewhere, surely? Downstairs, perhaps?

'OK, angel. Food first, then we're going to take you for a walk.'

Apple and custard went down like a charm, and Ariane's heart turned over at the child's smile when she lifted her from the high-chair.

'Fresh air,' she explained to Santos as she entered the kitchen with Christina balanced on one hip, 'together with a change of scene, is important for a child.'

'There's a pram in the storage room adjacent the garage. I'll fetch it and accompany you.'

She looked at him in disbelief. 'You're kidding, right? I don't intend going outside the grounds.'

'I'll enjoy the exercise.'

He wasn't going to budge. 'Aren't we getting just a little bit paranoid here?'

'So far, no photographs of Christina have reached the media. Manolo intends to keep it that way.'

In which case, a photograph would be worth a small fortune to whoever managed to take and sell that first shot.

'For how long?'

'Until there is some stability in her life.'

'Meantime, Christina is kept in isolation with no interaction with other children?' The words tumbled from her lips without thought. 'What he needs is a wife.'

Santos didn't miss a beat. 'I believe that has already occurred to him.'

Given there had to be a long line of women more than willing and able to fill such a position, all Manolo del Guardo had to do was make a selection!

Not her concern, Ariane assured silently. So why did her stomach twist into a painful knot at the thought?

'OK, let's organise the pram, and you can play bodyguard.' She even managed a smile.

The gardens were lovely, the air fresh and clean, and fine mosquito netting arranged over the pram served the dual purpose of keeping any flying insects at bay and a deterrent for any long-range photographic lens.

'You've been with your employer for a long time.'
Ariane framed it as an observation, and sensed
Santos' caution.

'Yes.'

'Based on a friendship that goes back to Manolo's
teen years in New York.'

'Yes.'

She spared him a musing glance as she navigated
the pathway. 'Monosyllabic answers do not a conversation make. I'm on my own time here, and just
for the record, the documentary on your boss is in the
can.'

'There is still the editing process.'

Ariane felt the beginnings of anger. Duplicity
wasn't her style. 'A fact which makes you wary in
case any additional information I manage to gain
could be added?'

His gaze was steady as it met hers. 'It's a possibility.'

'No,' she refuted quietly. 'It's not.'

The walked in silence, and it was several minutes
before Santos offered,

'Why not tell me something about yourself?'

'Every little detail is set down in a file Manolo
probably had you compile.'

'It's a necessary precaution,' Santos offered as they
traversed the driveway.

'Against old enemies who harbour a grudge?'
There had to be a few.

He shot her a measured look. 'Kidnapping and ransom. Manolo has little concern for his own safety. His daughter, however, is a different matter.'

A cellphone pealed, and Santos slid the unit from a pocket.

Manolo checking in? Ariane turned the pram and began retracing her steps, aware Santos followed a short distance behind her.

'Your car will be delivered in half an hour.' He caught her dark glance. 'Those were Manolo's instructions.'

How was it possible to feel grateful and resentful at the same time? Be gracious, a small voice advised. 'Thank you.'

Christina's bath-time was fun-filled with splashing, gurgling laughter, and went way over time simply because Ariane didn't have the heart to call short the babe's enjoyment.

Dinner waited until she'd fed and settled Christina for the night, and she took the solitary meal indoors, choosing to view television for a while before returning to her room.

She hadn't checked her cellphone since this morning, and tension began to build when she saw there were seven messages registered. Five from Roger, she determined, using different numbers. His tenacity in attempting to provoke and disturb raised her anger levels.

The words, no matter how she identified them as

coming from a sick mind, had the power to hurt. So much so, it took a few minutes for her to switch into control-mode.

There was no point in calling her parents or Alex; they'd only worry. The counsellor would only reiterate coping mechanisms, and she was familiar with all of them.

Friends, she had several, a few of whom were close enough to call at any time. Except they'd guess in an instant something was wrong, and demand she share coffee, a movie, anything, anywhere…and she wasn't free to do that.

Maybe if she went down to the kitchen and made a cup of tea, then collected one of several glossy magazines from the entertainment room…

No sooner had she made the tea when Santos strode into the kitchen, and the smile she summoned died at his serious expression. 'Is something wrong?'

'The security alarm has been activated.'

She hadn't heard a sound. 'Heat sensors, video surveillance,' he explained briefly.

Ariane stilled. 'Which indicates…?'

'An intruder in the grounds.'

She was already running. 'Christina—'

'No one has entered the house.'

Ariane didn't wait to ask how he knew that. Instead she moved quickly upstairs to the nursery.

It was a relief to see Christina sleeping peacefully

in her cot, and Ariane stood watching the child's steady breathing for a few long minutes.

She was an angelic-looking child, with such delicate features.

Given the hi-tech security covering the house and grounds, there would be the inevitable security callout, possibly the police, which Santos would handle.

Meantime she'd stay with Christina, and she settled into a comfortable chair.

CHAPTER FIVE

IT WAS there Manolo found her several hours later, and he stood watching the steady rise and fall of her breathing, the pale hair loosened. Her legs were tucked beneath her and her head resting against the armchair support.

It had been a hell of a day, he reflected wearily. The meetings had gone well. The exception was the appearance of Valentina Vaquez at the same restaurant where he'd shared lunch with a colleague.

An exasperated sigh issued from his lips. Valentina had connections, and she used them ruthlessly.

Her excuse was a shopping spree in Toorak, which didn't fool him at all. Worse, she'd turned up at the airport and not only shared his flight but also managed to gain the adjacent seat.

As if that weren't enough, she'd walked at his side to the car park and made it obvious she expected him to drive her home.

The seductive invitation to 'come in for coffee' when he drew the car to a halt outside her apartment had brought his polite refusal…something which didn't please the lady at all.

To top the night off, he'd had to deal with the aftermath of a home-invasion attempt.

What he needed was a stiff drink. Something he promised himself as he tugged off his loosened tie.

For a long moment he stood still as he took in the scene. His daughter was asleep…so, too, was Ariane.

There were two options…he could leave her where she was, or quietly wake her.

He chose the latter, and was totally unprepared for the speed with which she came out of the chair, fully alert in defensive mode.

Ariane felt hard hands clamp her wrists, and she kicked out with her feet, heard a faint grunt as her aim was deflected. In a matter of seconds she found herself being hauled over one male shoulder and carried from the room.

In the hallway she was unceremoniously lowered to her feet, and it was then she recognised her attacker.

Oh, God. Manolo del Guardo.

Her lips parted in silent dismay, then closed again. 'I'm sorry,' she managed at last. 'I thought—'

'I have to admire your style.'

She was still caught in the horror of her reaction. 'I'm sorry.'

The reiteration brought a wry smile. 'So you said.'

'Really, I didn't know it was you.'

'Quit while you're ahead.'

Ariane lifted a hand, then dropped it. 'Christina

slept through.' It was rare for her to be lost for words. 'We had a good day.'

'So I heard.'

She was locked into something she didn't under- stand. Maybe it was the lateness of the hour, Manolo's unexpected appearance...dammit, her in- stinctive reaction.

But something was happening here. She could sense it, *feel* it.

Her body swayed a little...fatigue maybe, or shock? Whatever, she lifted a hand as if to steady herself and felt his hands close over her shoulders.

'Easy now.' His voice was quiet, too quiet.

'I'm fine,' she said quickly as she sensed his con- cern. Hell, he thought she might faint. Something she never did.

She moved back a step. 'Was the intruder caught?'

Manolo let one hand drop. 'He fled over the wall. The surveillance cameras have his escapade on film. Not that it'll do much good. He wore a ski-mask.'

Ariane felt the blood drain from her face. Roger? Surely he wouldn't... 'I can view the surveillance tape.'

Manolo didn't pretend to misunderstand. 'The in- truder's build is smaller, the height estimate a few inches shorter than your ex-husband's recorded sta- tistics.'

Which could mean Roger might have hired someone to cause the disturbance. As a way to get at her? Or merely to show her that he could?

There was, of course, a possibility tonight had been an unrelated occurrence and he wasn't involved at all.

Sure, and pigs fly, a sceptical imp prompted silently.

If she had any sense, she'd go back to her apartment and her life. There, Roger's contact would reduce to the usual two or three daily messages. She didn't like it, but she dealt with it. At least then she wasn't endangering anyone else's peace of mind.

'No.'

Her chin tilted, and her eyes flew wide. 'Excuse me?'

'Don't play his game.'

'And you're an expert on psychological disorders?'

He'd witnessed the effects too often in the past. The anger, frustration, *rage* that led to uncontrollable behaviour.

It was late, he was tired, and this conversation wasn't going anywhere. 'Go to bed.'

Her eyes flared. 'Don't patronise me.'

She was bent on arguing with him? 'That wasn't my intention.'

Oh, hell, she was in danger of losing it. Her vision shimmered, and she blinked in rapid succession at his soft imprecation.

His hands framed her face, then his head lowered and his mouth closed over hers.

An action that surprised them both. Ariane didn't pull away, and neither did he.

Dear heaven, he was good at this. Just a few seconds, she promised herself. It's only a kiss. It doesn't mean anything.

Manolo didn't move, and neither did she, although the temptation to lean in to him was strong.

Move away now. The caution was a silent scream, and she tried to obey. Except it was too late, way too late as he deepened the kiss and coaxed her response.

No one had affected her quite like this. The warmth fanned to heat as her senses came to life with a vibrant radiance she found as startling as it was pleasurable.

Although *pleasure* didn't cover it. This was shooting stars and coloured rainbows…the entire galaxy.

And it had to stop before it got out of control.

Manolo felt her resistance and carefully eased her free.

Neither said a word as they stood transfixed for several seconds. He trailed gentle fingers down her cheek and lingered briefly at the edge of her mouth.

With a strangled sound Ariane turned and walked quickly along the gallery to her room, unaware he stood motionless until she was out of sight.

Hell, what was *that*?

What began as an impulsive need to soothe had become something else. If he wasn't so damn tired, he'd call it what it was…deep and meaningful.

Manolo moved into his suite, closed the door and began discarding his clothes. All too aware a certain part of his body was far from weary.

Forget the whisky and head for the shower…a leisurely one with the temperature dial for the last minute switched to cold.

There was no sign of Manolo when Ariane went down to breakfast, and she was immeasurably relieved when Santos revealed he'd already left for his city office.

Had he slept any better than she had? If she'd slept at all as she tossed and turned, analysing the *kiss* from so many angles it resembled a complex geometrical puzzle.

It had merely been a random impulsive act, she assured for the umpteenth time as she balanced orange juice and a plate with egg on toast in one hand and steaming black coffee in another.

Fresh air was a prime requisite, and she moved carefully out onto the terrace, then she settled down at the small table and attempted to do the food justice.

Two messages from Roger this morning, but neither gave any hint he might have been behind last night's intrusion.

Christina was a delight, smiling each time Ariane picked her up, chuckling and giggling as they played.

Any day soon it would end, she'd return to her own

life, and she'd never re-enter this house or have reason to see Manolo or his daughter again.

Consequently she made every moment count, and she chose to take her evening meal in the nursery on the pretext of spending time with Christina.

If she hoped the excuse would help her avoid Manolo, it didn't work, for she was just finishing off giving the babe her bottle when he entered the room.

All day she'd been in a state of fluctuating nerves, anticipating this particular moment. Which was ridiculous. She'd smile and simply act as normal. There was no need to feel awkward.

Yet there was nothing she could do about the way her pulse picked up speed at the sight of him. Or control the heat spreading throughout her body. All her fine body hairs seemed to stand on end, and as to the sensation swirling deep inside…let's not even go there.

From one kiss she'd taken a quantum leap to *this*?

It didn't make sense.

'Santos reports there were no problems through the day. No leads on the intruder.' His mouth curved into a warm smile as he reached for his daughter. 'And you, *pequeña*. The day has been good?'

Christina made a gurgling sound and pumped her legs as he cradled her close.

Ariane rose from the rocking chair and took a step towards the door, only to come to an abrupt halt as Manolo's hand closed over her arm.

'We need to talk.' His gaze caught and trapped hers.

'Christina is due to go down for the night in half an hour.' She swallowed the sudden lump that had risen in her throat. 'I have a few things to do while you spend some quality time with her.'

He took in the fast-beating pulse at the edge of her neck, and killed the urge to soothe it as he let her go.

Cool, she could do *cool*…for as long as it took to reach her room. Then and only then did her composure begin to shred.

Ariane checked her cellphone for messages…three from Roger in the usual obnoxious vein, one from Tony, 'just checking you're OK', and the last from her mother with a brief weekly update. Something she returned via SMS with 'everything fine this end. Love'. Tony received a similar response.

Manolo was in the process of tucking a light blanket over Christina's sleeping form when Ariane re-entered the nursery, and she hovered as he adjusted the night light before leading her from the room.

'We'll take this in my study.' He needed to shower and shave, eat, then spend serious time on the computer.

But first he wanted to get this out of the way, and he ushered her into the spacious book-lined room, indicated a chair, and crossed to the desk to lean one hip against the smooth polished wood.

'The agency rang to confirm they have a replacement nanny available to begin tomorrow morning.'

She should be relieved. 'I'll leave after breakfast.' Why did she have this sinking feeling in the pit of her stomach?

'Whenever is convenient,' Manolo indicated with a negligible lift of his shoulders.

It was for the best. She could walk away, get on with her life, and forget this interlude had ever taken place.

'I want to thank you for agreeing to fill in during the past few days.' He withdrew a cheque from his jacket pocket and extended it to her. 'A token of my gratitude for caring for my daughter.'

Ariane didn't move. 'I don't want your money.'

His eyes narrowed fractionally. 'We agreed—'

'No,' she corrected. 'You offered to pay me. I don't remember accepting.'

'Ariane—'

She stood to her feet and met his gaze with un-flinching regard. 'The television-programme manager will contact you when the documentary has been ed-ited. A copy will be couriered to you for your final approval as per your instructions.'

Pride...he recognised it, admired it. 'I'll have Santos mail the cheque.'

Her eyes sparked green fire. Since when had they been *green*? he mused, momentarily caught up with fascination. Her slender figure was straight, held with a dancer's poise...or a martial-art exponent's, poised for a killing move. Remembering her attack of the previous night, he was inclined towards the latter.

'Do that,' Ariane said quietly. 'And I'll return it unopened.'

There wasn't going to be a better exit line, and she turned and walked calmly from the room, closing the door behind her.

Tears were for the weak, and she resolutely refused to shed any. In her suite she turned her attention to packing, a process which took only minutes, then she gathered up her nightwear and headed into the *en suite* for a shower.

She cursed herself for a fool as she stood beneath the warm, pulsing spray, and reiterated the words on the edge of sleep.

Ariane woke at Christina's first early-morning cry, did the nappy change, then fed her bottled formula and settled the babe in the cot with a selection of soft toys while she returned to her room to dress.

The house was quiet, except for the faint baby noises emitting from the monitor, and she slipped back into the nursery to write up a schedule for the new nanny's benefit.

Last feed, last bottle, last play-time.

A few more hours, then she'd sling her bag in the boot of her car and drive away.

If only she could do it without having to face Manolo…yet the deity took no notice of her plea.

Act, she admonished silently. Smile. Pretend nothing had happened, and the kiss was merely a figment of her imagination.

Fat chance! All it took was one look at him when he entered the nursery for her to vividly recall how it felt to have his mouth on her own.

Freshly shaven, his hair damp from a recent shower, attired in black tailored trousers and a dark blue business shirt unbuttoned at the neck, he looked the powerful, dynamic man he was portrayed to be. He wore the mantle well, with a primitive edge that many coveted but few possessed.

As a lover, he would know all the moves, which buttons to push, where the stroke of his tongue was more effective than a finger's touch.

Without doubt he had the sensual skill to drive a woman wild. What was more, he'd use that expertise to send her to the edge, hold her there, then catch her as she fell.

Dammit, what was the matter with her?

'Good morning.' Amazing…her voice sounded calm, normal.

Did his gaze linger a little too long as he returned the greeting? She hoped not. 'I'll go have breakfast while you spend time with Christina.'

He didn't attempt to stop her, and minutes later she entered the kitchen, snagged a banana from the fruit bowl, caught up the day's newspaper and took both out onto the terrace.

The sun's warmth caressed her skin as she tried to focus on the headlines, but all she saw was jumbled print as she scanned the page.

The banana was probably succulent, but it could have been sawdust for all the notice her tastebuds took.

'You forgot to get coffee.'

She glanced up as Santos deposited a cup of aromatic black brew onto the table. 'Thanks.'

He paused, then continued quietly, 'You will stay until the nanny arrives?'

'What time is she expected?'

'Around nine, I believe.'

'OK.' So she'd stay, say 'hi', hand over the feeding schedule, then leave.

The coffee was hot, and she added sugar, then sipped it as she pretended interest in the daily news.

How long did Manolo spend with his daughter each morning? Fifteen minutes? Twenty? Which meant he'd be down for breakfast any time soon.

If she could manage to avoid him, all the better.

She almost made it, only to misjudge his presence by a few seconds as she passed through the kitchen.

'You've been an excellent host.' She met his gaze, and offered a smile. 'Thank you.' Politeness was something her parents had taught her from a young age.

'My pleasure.'

Another few nights beneath his roof and she might

become his pleasure. Something that would be the antithesis of wisdom!

'Christina is due for her cereal.'

Did he see it for the escape it was? Oh, for heaven's sake! As if she should care...except she did. Too much.

The new nanny arrived precisely at nine, which Ariane took as an omen from her vantage point in the kitchen. Punctuality was good.

Within minutes Santos ushered the woman into the kitchen and effected an introduction.

The nurse's uniform, complete with sensible flat shoes, cap, provided an efficient persona.

A cry emitted through the monitor, and from then on it was all downhill as Santos led the way to the nursery with, at the nanny's insistence, Ariane trailing close behind.

'It's beneficial for the outgoing nanny to introduce the new nanny to the child.'

Ariane wasn't so sure as Christina burst into voluble protest.

'If you'll pick her up and hand her to me, she'll understand I'm now in charge.'

'Her name is Christina,' Ariane reminded quietly.

'Yes, of course.'

Christina sobbed in earnest, her baby features becoming more red by the second.

'I don't think this is a good idea,' Ariane ventured, and incurred the nanny's haughty glance.

'I'm the professional here.'

Indisputably, but what about some understanding…and hell, an attempt at affection?

Christina's voice rose in crescendo, her dark eyes moving from one adult to the other in desperation.

Ariane met Santos' masked gaze and held it for a few seconds, then she reached into the cot and gathered Christina close. The cries subsided into heart-rending hiccups as the small body shuddered, then clung.

'You'll find Christina's feeding schedule on the credenza.' Ariane tried for normalcy and almost didn't make it. 'Clothes, nappies, supplies…' She indicated built-in nursery furniture. 'Christina is due for her bottle, then she'll nap for a few hours.'

The nanny checked her watch. 'Hmm. The schedule needs some adjusting.' She offered a practised smile. 'Give me the child.' The smile switched to Santos. 'You can arrange for my bags to be brought up, and when the child is fed you can show me my accommodation.' The smile disappeared as she took Christina. 'It's better if you both go now. The child and I need to become acquainted.'

'The child' screamed.

Ariane wanted to gather Christina close and instruct the nanny to return from whence she'd come. Except she didn't have the right.

Christina's cries echoed in decreasing volume as Ariane descended the stairs at Santos' side.

Was Santos aware of her inner struggle to contain the silent tears shimmering beneath the surface? Were they visible? Dear heaven, she hoped not.

Her bag was already stowed in the boot of her car in the garage. All she had to do was bid Santos 'goodbye', then slip behind the wheel of the BMW and drive away.

A few words, a shaky smile, then she cleared the driveway and passed through the open gates.

Did hearts break? A week ago she would have disputed such a claim. Now, she wasn't so sure.

CHAPTER SIX

THERE was nothing to be gained by languishing in the apartment, Ariane determined soon after her return. Household chores took precedence, and when they were done she contacted friends, arranging get-togethers over coffee, lunch, dinner, attending the movies... The deal being to fill her days and evenings, leaving her little time to *think*.

It worked...almost.

She made it through to Sunday, and spent the day with a group of friends cruising the inner harbour. Daylight-saving summer time allowed for a barbecue in a nearby park, and it was almost nine when she was dropped off outside her apartment building.

'Bye; thanks for the lift.' She stepped onto the kerb and watched the car move forward, then she made her way to the main entrance feeling pleasantly light-hearted after a fun-filled day made all the more carefree without the intrusion of pager or cellphone.

On entering her apartment she had no other thought than to take a shower, watch a television show, then grab an early night.

The answering-machine was blinking, with the digital recorder registering seven messages.

Three from Roger came as no surprise, and were repetitively abhorrent as usual. She wanted to retaliate with *get a life*, except there was no point talking to an inanimate machine.

One from Tony, bless him, suggesting they share a pizza through the week; her mother; her brother, Alex.

The last was from Santos, and Ariane pressed 're-wind' to double-check the number he requested she call.

For a brief moment she hesitated, then she picked up the receiver and dialled.

Santos answered on the third ring, and after a brief greeting he relayed, 'I'll transfer you.'

Her heart began to race, and she gripped the receiver as Manolo came on the line.

'Ariane. Can we meet this evening?'

The sound of his voice sent goose-pimples scudding down her spine. What could he possibly want that had to be *tonight*? 'I don't think—'

'An hour. Coffee. I'll collect you. Shall we say fifteen minutes?'

Hell. Her skin held sun-screen-lotion residue, there was sea-spray in her hair... 'Half an hour. I'll meet you at the apartment entrance. It's—'

'I know where it is.'

The connection was cut before she could utter a further word.

Christina, the nanny...had to be, she reasoned as

she hit the shower and washed her hair. If he wanted her to fill in as a nanny substitute again, she didn't think she could do it.

To be in the same house, so acutely aware of him, would be madness. It would be best if she rang and cancelled out of meeting him. Yet he was probably already on his way...

Dammit, why hadn't she thought to refuse seeing him? Because he took you unawares and didn't give you a chance to think!

So, she'd have coffee and tell him she wasn't interested in whatever it was he intended to propose. How hard would it be?

Towelled dry, she hurriedly pulled on fresh underwear, added tailored trousers and a cotton-knit top, then she slipped her feet into stilettos, swept her damp hair into a careless knot, added a touch of colour to her lips, caught up keys, purse, and exited her apartment with scant minutes to spare.

Manolo was waiting for her outside the main entrance, his tall frame clearly visible as she entered the main lobby.

Even through thick plate-glass doors he managed to project a disturbing aura of power. Combined with primal sexual chemistry, the mix had a devastating effect on the female equilibrium. Especially hers.

Warm, friendly, polite. She could do all three as a practised art form. It was integral to her personality, and part of her job.

'My car is over there.' He indicated a sleek Aston Martin in the guest parking bay, and she fell into step at his side.

In the close confines of the car she was far too aware of him, the faint musky tang of his exclusive cologne, the sheer sexual energy he managed to exude without any effort at all.

It was crazy to be so conscious of every breath she took, the quickened beat of her heart, and the warmth flooding through her body.

She retained a vivid memory of how it felt to have his mouth possess her own, the taste and feel of it, the exploratory touch. She'd had to fight against the urge to take it closer, deeper...

Instead, they'd lingered a little, then drawn apart.

Which was just as well, she qualified as she watched the night-scene unfold as Manolo entered trendy Double Bay.

The boutique-café scene was alive and well, and she looked askance as he eased the car to a halt outside the entrance to the classy, upmarket Ritz Carlton Hotel.

The concierge almost made a salaam to him in recognition, and summoned a porter to take care of Manolo's car.

Doors were opened, greetings exchanged, and Ariane kept her lips sealed as they entered the foyer.

Not their destination, she determined as he led her

towards a private lounge and indicated a table and two comfortable chairs.

'Coffee,' Ariane requested as a waiter moved swiftly towards them.

Manolo gave their order, then he settled back in the chair with indolent ease and regarded her steadily. 'I prefer some degree of privacy.'

It made sense, given the number of patrons occupying the numerous pavement cafés close by.

The waiter returned with their coffee, and made a production of setting out sugar and cream, plus a complimentary serving of petits fours.

Ariane added sugar, deferred on the cream, and stirred. It was a long time since she'd felt lost for conversation. But hell, what did they have to discuss? The weather?

She lifted a hand and gestured towards their coffee. 'Perhaps you could get to the reason for all this?'

He took his time spooning sugar into his cup. 'There has to be a reason?'

Ariane couldn't imagine him doing anything without calculated forethought. 'Yes,' she said simply, and caught his faint smile.

'Perceptive of you.' He lifted his cup and took a measured sip, then lowered it down onto the saucer.

'You returned my cheque.'

Ariane held his gaze as she offered slowly, 'Did you imagine I wouldn't?'

Had it been part of a game-play? He withdrew the

cheque from his pocket and placed it onto the table. 'I insist you accept it.'

Ariane restrained the urge to hit him. Instead she leaned forward, picked up the cheque, then she calmly tore it in two and returned the pieces to the table.

Indolent amusement pulled at the edges of his mouth. 'I can write out another.'

'I didn't look after Christina because you offered to pay me.' She had to ask, 'How is she?'

His expression remained unchanged, although his gaze narrowed slightly, causing the tiny lines fanning out from his eyes to become more pronounced. 'Christina hasn't settled since you left.'

Regret clouded her eyes as she controlled the sudden shaft of pain. Poor little mite. 'I'm sorry to hear that.'

'Yes, I believe you are.' A rueful smile tugged the edges of his mouth. 'The nanny walked. The implication being Christina is a difficult child requiring specialised care.'

'What rubbish.' The words slipped out before she gave them thought. 'Christina needs someone constant in her life. A string of nannies isn't going to cut it for her.'

'I agree.' His expression became contemplative. 'The only satisfactory solution is for me to remarry and provide her with a mother figure.'

Now, why did that suggestion make her feel ill?

Fool, she derided silently. Where did you think one kiss would lead? 'Congratulations.'

'A little premature,' Manolo drawled. 'I've yet to ask the lady.'

Ariane leaned back in her chair and endeavoured to deal with the way her blood seemed to chill in her veins. 'Whoever she is, I doubt she'll refuse.'

His smile held a marked degree of cynicism. 'Based on the assumption I can provide her with a diamond-studded meal ticket?'

'Most women would consider it a major incentive.'

'But not you?'

She'd seen first-hand what acquired wealth could do. Mostly it wasn't pretty. 'Wealth and possessions aren't the most important things in life.'

'Spoken by someone who has never had to be without them.'

'My parents showed enough wisdom to provide Alex and me with everything we needed, as well as some of the things we wanted. Anything else we were taught to work for.'

Manolo inclined his head in deference. 'So, what, in your opinion, is important?'

She didn't have to think. 'Loyalty, integrity. Love,' she added.

He studied her thoughtfully. 'I wasn't around when they were being handed out.' He drained his coffee-cup, then set it to one side. 'Do your ex-husband's nuisance calls remain a problem?'

'I don't see the relevance.'

'Humour me.'

'Specifics?' Her gaze speared his with unflinching disregard. 'In a twenty-four-hour time-frame, it can vary between seven to ten intrusions via text messages, voice mail, my answering-machine.' Sometimes more, depending on the interviewee and work environment.

'I imagine you're aware that your position as a television presenter ensures you're constantly accessible to him via the screen?'

'So is everyone else who appears behind the television camera.'

'Except they're not his obsession.'

'No.'

'Do you perceive embarking on another career direction?'

She met the queries head-on. 'Such as?'

'Marriage.'

'Doubtful. Why repeat a mistake?'

'Not even for the security marriage would provide?'

'A partner at social functions?' Ariane took it to the next level. 'The pleasure of intimacy?'

Manolo's expression didn't change. 'Is it the former or latter which has little appeal?'

Oh, my. 'I don't think I need to answer that.'

'What of a family? Don't children enter your equation?'

Pain twisted deep inside. 'I've considered adopting as a single mother. Although I'd have to continue working. Which would mean nursery daycare, a nanny. It doesn't seem fair to the child.'

'We agree Christina needs a mother. I'm proposing you take on that role.'

It got her attention, as it was meant to do.

'As my wife,' Manolo added, to clarify any misunderstanding.

She just looked at him. 'You're insane.'

'Am I?' He trapped her gaze.

'Why *marriage*?'

'I want some permanence in my daughter's life. Someone who'll love and care for her as if she's her own. Christina bonded with you, as you did with her.'

'Therefore I'd be an ideal choice?' Ariane queried carefully.

'You'll benefit financially with a marital agreement paying you two million dollars for every year you remain my wife. Together with credit-card facilities to an annual total of two million dollars. Gifts, jewellery, will be an added bonus. A pre-nuptial agreement will pay you a handsome settlement should we divorce.'

'And in return, you get a mother for your child, a social hostess, and a woman in your bed.' She could feel the anger simmering just beneath the surface. 'All tied up in a business deal.'

'It's an attractive package.'

'You were doing just fine until you mentioned agreements and deals.' She stood to her feet, and for a brief moment it felt good to have the height advantage over him.

A hand closed over her wrist. 'I'm not done yet.'

His grip didn't tighten, but she had the feeling it would if she attempted to wrench her arm free.

'Please,' he said quietly. 'Sit down and hear me out.'

'Manolo—'

'Christina needs you in her life.'

Nerves skittered a path down her spine as she sank down into the chair. 'Any caring woman will do.'

'*You,*' he insisted with dangerous softness. 'I'm offering the security of a convenient marriage based on friendship and mutual respect.'

Lovers and friends. The mere thought of having him as a lover sent her emotions spiralling out of control.

'You gain a mother for Christina, while I gain a much-wanted daughter. No false hopes or illusions,' Ariane concluded, and glimpsed his slight smile.

'Precisely.'

Could she do it? *Dared she?*

'Can I have time to think about it?'

'I'll contact you tomorrow.'

Her heart lurched and didn't really settle. 'There's just one thing.'

His expression remained unchanged. 'Yes?'

'I have my own money.' She drew in a deep breath and slowly released it. 'I don't want or need yours.' Dear lord, she had to get out of here. If she stayed any longer she'd dissolve into an emotional puddle. 'There's no need for you to leave. I'll take a cab.'

He extracted a note, tucked it beneath a saucer, then rose to his feet. 'I'll drive you home.'

'I'd rather you didn't.' She stepped away from the table and walked through to the main foyer, where she had the concierge summon a cab.

She didn't look back to see if Manolo followed, and it wasn't until she reached her apartment that she gave in to her emotions.

Ariane slept badly, and woke nursing a headache.

Hardly surprising, given Manolo's shock proposal, she rationalised as she dressed for work.

Traffic snarls at this hour of the morning were the norm, and she entered the television-channel head-quarters with few minutes to spare.

The morning quickly digressed into the day from hell. After a week's break there was a backlog of paperwork requiring her attention, calls to make and information to chase. Everything needed to be done yesterday, and she stayed late in an attempt to create some sort of order from the day's chaos.

Consequently it was almost seven when she exited the building and crossed to the staff car park.

Home, a long, cool drink, a shower, something to

eat were on her list of priorities. As to the rest of the evening…she should put in an hour or two on the laptop.

Ariane reached into her bag to retrieve her keys, and when she glanced up it was to see Manolo emerging from the car parked next to her own.

Surprise held her immobile for a few timeless seconds as she held his gaze.

The black business suit, dark blue shirt and matching silk tie merely enhanced the elemental ruthlessness he managed to exude without any effort at all.

'Bad day?' His drawling voice was lacking in cynicism, and she offered a faint smile.

'Like you wouldn't believe.'

He took in her pale features, the darkness of her eyes, and offered quietly, 'Have you eaten?'

Food? The last time she remembered eating was a sandwich around midday. 'No.'

'Neither have I. Your car or mine?'

'I don't think—'

'A restaurant, café, preferably somewhere quiet, or we grab take-out and go eat it in a park.'

Couldn't he see she was beat? 'Manolo—'

'Indulge me.'

'There's a place not far from here.' Somewhere she often stopped off when she worked late. 'It's probably easier if you follow me in your car.'

He removed the keys from her hand, unlocked the car door, then handed them back to her. The warm brush of his fingers against her own was electric, and she was unaware of holding her breath until she slid in behind the wheel.

All day she'd compiled a mental list of the reasons *for* and *against* marrying Manolo del Guardo, and come up with the definitive answer she'd be mad not to give.

Each time the phone had rung she imagined it would be him, and, given her workload, by day's end she was a mess.

It didn't take long to reach the small family-owned Italian restaurant in a neighbouring suburb, and within minutes they were seated at a table, the menu produced and their order given.

The cosy atmosphere held a friendly warmth, and Ariane fought against her awareness of the man seated close by.

He emanated inherent vitality with ease, yet beneath the sophisticated façade there was a hint of the primitive.

'Your first day back at work, and everything went to hell in a handbasket?'

'Is it that obvious?'

No man with any *nous* told a woman she looked tired or stressed without being able to do something about it. 'A natural assumption, given you worked late.'

Ariane took a long sip of chilled water, then nibbled on the excellent bruschetta the waiter placed before them. It was followed soon after with two plates of steaming food…ambrosia, she determined as she speared her fork into the tortellini.

'Eat first,' Manolo bade as he caught the rapid pulse-beat in the hollow of her throat.

'Meanwhile we aim for polite conversation?'

The edges of his mouth lifted. 'Something like that.'

'OK. You can begin by filling me in on your day.'

'Meetings in Adelaide this morning, followed by a consult in the city this afternoon.'

'Another high-powered business deal successfully cemented?'

'Yes.'

A few minutes later Ariane slid her empty plate to one side, refused dessert and requested tea.

'Have you taken anything for that headache?'

He couldn't know she'd been battling it all day. 'Nothing strong enough. When I go home, I'll take a couple of pills, then crawl into bed.'

The waiter removed their plates, then returned minutes later with tea and coffee.

'You've given my proposal sufficient thought?'

The moment she'd mentally agonised over had arrived.

'Yes.'

'And?'

'I accept your proposal. With a few conditions,' she added.

'Perhaps you'd care to run them by me?'

'I'll accept a reasonable monthly allowance.'

A smile tugged his mouth. 'We already covered that.'

'A fraction of the amount you specified is more than adequate.'

'Go on.'

'I'll sign a pre-nup protecting your assets. They rightfully belong to Christina. Should we divorce, you provide me with a home and sufficient financial means of support.'

It had been taken care of. 'There's more?'

'You'll have my fidelity. I expect yours in return.'

'That's a given.'

'Your turn.'

'I've arranged a celebrant, who, at her discretion, is prepared to waive the usual waiting period and conduct our marriage ceremony at home on Friday.'

It was just as well she was sitting down. '*This* Friday?'

'A small private affair.'

'You're kidding me, right?'

'I'm perfectly serious.'

'But—' Three *days*. Four, if you counted Friday. It couldn't be done.

'Yes, it can.'

He was adept at reading her mind. 'My job—'

'Leave it with me.'

'*Friday?*' Ariane reiterated in disbelief.

'I'll set the legal paperwork in motion. Santos will help organise all the necessary details regarding your apartment, packers, storage facilities. It will simplify things if you move into the house on Thursday. Or before, if you get done ahead of time.'

Her head began to whirl at the thought of what she'd need to achieve. A roller-coaster ride didn't begin to describe it. 'This is happening too fast.'

'Trust me. It'll all come together.'

CHAPTER SEVEN

THE fact that it did owed much to Santos' skilled organisation. Each day had become filled with so much activity, it was often midnight before Ariane fell into bed, only to rise at dawn and start over again.

As to family…a promised visit by her parents for Christmas made up for the fact they were unable to attend at such short notice, and Alex arrived from Hong Kong Friday morning for a twenty-four-hour stopover before flying back the next day.

Choosing what to wear had been a dilemma, and after much deliberation she'd selected a simple sheath in ivory silk organza, matching stilettos, added a pearl pendant, pearl ear-studs, and swept her hair into a neat twist.

Now there was something magical about stepping slowly down the curving staircase at her brother's side.

No time for second thoughts, Ariane concluded silently as she locked gazes with the man waiting for her at the foot of the stairs.

Not that she had any doubts. Just a severe case of nerves, given she was minutes away from exchanging *Celeste* for *del Guardo*.

Standing tall, his broad-shouldered frame attired in black Armani, white shirt and silk tie, Manolo was something else, and the breath caught in her throat as he took her hand and threaded his fingers through her own.

Floral displays in pastel colours on an ornate tiered stand formed a beautiful background for the small linen-covered table where the celebrant stood in preparation for the intimate civil ceremony.

Santos, resplendent in a fine dark tailored suit, held Christina, and together with Alex both men acted as witnesses to the charming but simple exchange of vows.

Ariane was unprepared for the two rings Manolo placed on her finger, a diamond baguette-styled wedding band together with a magnificent pear-shaped diamond engagement ring. Surprise followed with a contoured gold wedding band for her to place on Manolo's left hand.

His faint smile as her fingers shook over the task almost undid her, and was compounded by the brief touch of his mouth on her own.

Get a grip. There's nothing special about this. It's merely a legality cementing a union of mutual convenience.

Yet tonight she'd share his bed. Something that had become more unnerving with each passing day. Now it was only a matter of hours away…

There was celebratory champagne, and following

the celebrant's departure Ariane took time out to feed Christina and put her down for the night before returning downstairs to share a sumptuous meal with Alex and Santos, prepared by a chef hired for the occasion.

Manolo was a practised host, with Santos almost his equal, Ariane determined as she ate a few morsels from each course, sipped superb champagne whilst attempting to catch up with her brother.

'Twenty-four hours isn't long enough,' she protested as the leisurely meal progressed. 'You could at least stay the weekend.'

'Sweetheart, as much as I adore you, there's a time and place for sibling togetherness, and,' Alex teased, 'this isn't it. Besides,' he added gently, 'the parents will be here for Christmas, and I can take a mid-year break.' His eyes sparkled with humour. 'I'll be back.'

'You will, of course, stay with us,' Manolo drawled, and Alex inclined his head in acceptance.

'Thanks.'

It was a while before they took coffee in the lounge. The chef quietly cleaned up and left, and Santos chose to retire to his quarters. Far too soon Alex rose to his feet and declared his intention to take a cab to a hotel close to the airport where he was taking an early-morning flight back to Hong Kong.

Ariane felt the tug of emotions as she hugged him when the cab drew in to the front entrance. His visit had been so brief, so very special.

'Love you,' she said softly, and felt the increased pressure as he pulled her close.

'You, too.'

Then he shook Manolo's hand and slid into the cab. Within seconds all she could see were the red tail-lights as the vehicle traversed the drive, then cleared the gates.

The day and everything it represented was over. Yet there was still the night, and her nerves began to shred at the thought.

Manolo locked up and set the security system, then he turned towards her. 'More coffee? Champagne?'

'No. Thanks,' Ariane added, wondering if he had a clue as to how she felt. 'I'll go check Christina.'

He shrugged off his jacket and loosened his tie. 'We'll both go.'

What time was it? Eleven? Midnight? *Did it matter?*

She was supremely conscious of him as they ascended the stairs, and in the nursery he seemed far too close as they stood silently watching the sleeping babe.

The master suite was at the end of the gallery. It was where her clothes were now stored in a capacious walk-in wardrobe. Her cosmetics and toiletries took up space on one half of the long marble-topped vanity with its double basins.

Even so, she had yet to share his room, his bed, and now that it was about to happen she shrank from

being accorded the failure Roger had frequently ac-
cused her of being.

Failure to please him, failure to give him a child.
Failure as a wife, a woman. At least he hadn't been
able to demean her career.

For the past few days Roger's ability to reach her
had diminished, for she no longer required a pager or
an answering-machine. His only avenue of harassment was via voice-mail and message-bank on her
cellphone. A fact which heightened the level of his
invective in the messages he left.

'You've had a hectic few days,' Manolo offered as
they entered the master suite, and Ariane's pulse
tripped its beat as she inclined her head.

Hectic was an understatement. 'Yes.' A movement
of her hand resulted in prisms of multicoloured light
shooting from the rings he'd placed there several
hours before. Gifts she had yet to acknowledge.

'The rings...' She paused fractionally. Oh, dear
heaven, was that her voice? It sounded distinctly
shaky. 'They're beautiful. Thank you.'

'My pleasure.'

A pleasure he would soon take. Maybe tonight she
could plead a headache and delay the inevitable. Who
was she kidding? Worse, what was the point?

He pulled off his tie and deftly undid his shirt buttons, then he pulled the shirt free and dropped it onto
a nearby chair.

Ariane felt her eyes widen at the superb musculature of his upper body. He worked out. Had to, she perceived, to gain that degree of fitness.

He slid off his shoes, removed his socks, and she was galvanised into movement when he reached for the fastening of his trousers.

'I'll go remove my make-up.' Then she turned and all but fled into the *en suite*.

Her nightgown and robe were where she'd placed them that morning, and she stepped out of her stilettos, shed her clothes, slipped on the satin sheath, then she covered it with the robe before cleansing her face.

OK, she could do this. A deep breath, then she opened the door and re-entered the bedroom.

Manolo emerged into the room at the same time, and at her surprise he indicated a second *en suite*. His.

'Oh, I thought…' she began, then stopped.

'We'd share?'

A towel hung low over his hips, and she deliberately fixed her gaze on his right shoulder as she aimed for a negligent shrug.

'You have no need to be nervous.'

His voice was a quiet drawl, and she cursed the soft colour flooding her cheeks. She lifted a hand, then let it fall. 'I'm not,' she faltered, then managed unevenly, 'terribly good at this.'

One eyebrow lifted, then his eyes narrowed as he examined her expression. Was this an act, or had the infamous Roger done a number on her? Somehow he suspected it was the latter.

He moved slowly towards her and paused within touching distance. 'Said who?' When she didn't answer, he queried softly, 'Your ex?'

Oh, lord, maybe if she closed her eyes, when she opened them again she'd discover this was just a dream.

No such luck. 'I wasn't able to satisfy him.' There, she'd said it.

Manolo lifted a hand and brushed light fingers down her cheek, watching as those beautiful green eyes darkened at his touch.

'Really?' He began removing the pins from her hair, then he threaded his fingers through its length and settled his hands on her shoulders.

Slowly, with infinite care, he lowered his head and brushed his lips to her temple, lingered there, then trailed a gentle path to the edge of her mouth.

The musky scent of his skin teased her senses, and warmth unfurled deep within as he traced her lips with his own, coaxing them to part, then when they did his tongue began a subtle exploration in what became a slow, erotic dance.

It was like no kiss she'd ever experienced, a seductive, provocative tasting that filled her senses and brought a soft sigh from her throat.

Ariane was unaware of her robe sliding free to fall in a heap at her feet, and she gave an audible gasp as his lips trailed to the edge of her neck, nuzzled there, then slid down to caress the hollow at the base of her throat, suckled a little before tracing a path to the soft swell of her breast.

Heat swelled deep inside and swirled through her body at his touch, and she gasped as he eased the shoestring straps over her shoulders, and let the satin slither to the carpet.

'Manolo—'

His mouth closed over one tender peak and savoured it, gently at first, then he stroked the swollen bud with his tongue. When he began to suckle, she cried out against the sudden sensation spiralling from deep within, and in an unbidden movement she took hold of his head and raked her fingers through his hair.

Just as she thought she couldn't take any more, he shifted position and rendered a similar treatment to its twin, only for her to cry out and beg for him to stop.

He complied, sliding up to claim her mouth in a deep kiss that verged close to possession.

She was burning up, so close to letting go that it came as a shock to feel the mattress beneath her back, and she stilled, caught up in the familiar sense of imminent failure.

Manolo's hands soothed, then began to stroke as he played her with a virtuoso's touch. Then he moved, his mouth following the path of his fingers with an aching slowness that made her want to beg.

He caressed every inch of her until she thought

she'd go mad, and she cried out as he rendered the most intimate kiss of all, stroking, teasing the sensitised clitoris until she went up and over in a burst of indescribable emotion.

It didn't stop, and warm tears filled her eyes, then spilled to trickle in slow rivulets across each temple to become lost in her hair.

Liquid fire coursed through her body until she became consumed by the flame, and it was then he rose over her, entering in one slow thrust that stretched silken tissues as he eased his way deep inside.

Dear heaven, he was big, filling her as Roger never had, and she gasped as he began to withdraw, only to cry out as he thrust even deeper.

In a rhythm as old as time, he took her places she'd never been before, soothing when her body shook in the throes of orgasm, and he held her as she fell, withholding his own pleasure until she scaled the heights again, then he joined her in an explosive climax, held her there, then shared a glorious free-fall that left them both spent.

Ariane couldn't move. Even to lift a finger seemed impossible. As to being able to utter a word…it was beyond her.

Manolo shifted to one side, then leaned towards her. It was then he saw the sheen of unshed tears, the faint evidence of those she'd already shed, and he lowered his mouth to hers in a lingering kiss.

Something twisted inside him. There was no artifice, no contrivance. What she'd gifted him had been genuine emotion.

He lifted his head and took in the pale features, the exhaustion apparent, and he slid from the bed and filled the spa-bath.

Minutes later he lifted her into his arms and carried her into the *en suite*.

'What are you doing?'

'Indulging you.'

He stepped into the bath, set her down, joined her, then activated the jets.

It was heaven, and she leaned back, eyes closed as the warm water worked its magic.

She felt…dear heaven, how did she feel? As if she was floating, she decided dreamily. Warm, sensually sated, relaxed to the point of inertia. Inwardly still coming to terms with what she'd experienced in Manolo's bed.

So *this* was the motivation for songwriters' and poets' eloquence and angst. And she'd thought it was merely the stuff of romantic fiction, actors portraying a part, and, from her own experience, vastly overrated.

'Thank you.' The words were so softly spoken Manolo had to lean forward to hear them.

'For what, specifically?'

'Showing me the difference,' Ariane said simply.

Light fingers trailed her cheek, lingered, then he

switched off the jets and stood to his feet. 'You need to sleep.'

She didn't want to move. Except the comfort of bed was a persuasive option, and she followed his actions, snagged a towel, then she dried off and fastened the towel around her slim form.

It would be nice to reach his comfort zone, ignore convention and walk into the bedroom naked…as he did.

He was something else, with a physical stature most men would die for. Great butt, muscular thighs, lean hips.

A street warrior, risen from a poor neighbourhood where survival and staying one step ahead of the law were the only criteria.

It made for a tough, ruthless quality he hid well beneath a sophisticated façade, acquired during his rise through the social ranks to become the man he was today.

Except the core of the man remained, buried beneath the surface, and she suppressed a faint shiver as she shed the towel and slid between the bedcovers.

'Cold?'

Just a nebulous ghost passing by. 'No.'

Warm hands reached for her as he pulled her in against him. 'Sleep, hmm.'

She felt his lips touch her hair, and she closed her eyes.

It was good, better than good to lie here like this. He'd been kind, more than kind.

She was his wife, stepmother to his child. And the sex was great. A wonderful unexpected bonus.

But don't confuse *good* and *kind* with a deeper emotion, she warned, close to the edge of sleep. Love wasn't part of the bargain they'd struck, and only a fool would imagine otherwise.

CHAPTER EIGHT

'MANOLO received a call early this morning,' Santos relayed when Ariane entered the kitchen for breakfast. 'A London colleague has a five-hour stopover. He'll be absent most of the day.'

What did you expect? a tiny voice taunted. That after a night of great sex…make that cataclysmic lovemaking…he'd be lying next to you when you woke, take you on another wild, passionate roller-coaster ride, then promise you another sensual feast tonight?

Get real. This was reality, not fantasy.

While she might feel as if she'd discovered the pot of sensual gold at the end of a rainbow, he probably felt disappointed at her saddening lack of sexual experience.

Coffee. She needed it hot, strong and sweet.

'Manolo asked me to let you know there's a long-standing fund-raiser event scheduled for this evening which you'll both attend. Formal wear.' He named a prestigious inner-city hotel. 'If you could be ready to leave at seven.' He anticipated her question and answered before she had an opportunity to voice it. 'I will be on hand if Christina should wake.'

114

Twenty-four hours after marrying him, and she was being thrust into the glare of the social limelight. *Great.*

'I imagine it's out of the question Manolo will go alone?'

'It's not a consideration.'

In that case, some personal pampering was in store. She also needed to decide what to wear. There was also the necessity to juggle Christina's evening bottle.

Something Santos took care of, leaving Ariane free to shower and dress.

Manolo was in the process of fixing his shirt when she emerged from the *en suite*, and her heart-rate tripped, then sped up to a faster beat.

For a few timeless seconds her eyes locked with his, and she was willing to swear she forgot to breathe.

He was something else. Shaped by his youth, and empowered by the transition, there was an exigent masculinity apparent, a powerful sexual alchemy that was dangerously primitive.

Last night…let's not go there. The thought she might share a similar sexual feast tonight almost brought her undone.

Dress, she commanded silently. She'd already tended to her make-up, her hair. All she had to do was slip into her gown, step into stilettos, add jewellery…

Chiffon silk in a symphony of soft florals, with

asymmetric lines and a delicate frill on one side. Shoestring straps and a scooped, draped neckline enhanced its sophisticated flair, and she added a long wrap in matching silk.

'You're throwing me in at the deep end,' Ariane stated as she fixed ear-studs in place, then added a bracelet.

'I've had the tickets for several weeks,' Manolo informed as he slid them into his jacket pocket, and followed them with his cellphone.

'Which woman am I supplanting?'

His eyes narrowed slightly. 'That doesn't enter the equation.'

Perhaps not, except he would have taken a partner, and she wondered *who*, given his appearance in various glossy magazines with a number of different women at such events in the past.

OK, she assured silently as she collected her evening purse. She was as ready as she'd ever be to face whatever the evening held.

'Shall we leave?'

She sounded calm, but Manolo caught the tell-tale fast-beating pulse in the hollow at the base of her throat… Not so cool, after all.

A quick peek into the nursery provided reassurance, a final check with Santos, then minutes later Manolo eased the Aston Martin through the gates.

It was a pleasant evening, the light beginning to fade slightly as night drew close. Soon the streetlights would come on, and flashing neon on city buildings blaze in a colourful display.

Tonight's fund-raiser was organised to benefit a children's charity. Attendance by several of the city's social élite was considered *de rigueur*.

There was no reason for her to feel nervous. She'd appeared in the public spotlight as part of her job. Out of it, she'd attended her share of social activities.

What was more, tonight she had Manolo at her side. Maybe that was part of the problem, she mused as he drew the car to a halt at the hotel entrance and handed the keys to the porter for valet parking.

Smile, *act*, she bade silently as they took the lift to the grand ballroom, where a number of guests were gathered in the adjacent foyer enjoying proffered champagne.

Manolo's appearance garnered attention, and Ariane's presence caused covert speculation of a kind she'd have preferred to do without.

'Darling. There you are,' a soft feminine voice purred in welcome, and Ariane turned slowly to face a tall, svelte woman with long, flowing dark hair that fell almost to her waist, porcelain skin, perfect make-up.

Her features were familiar, so was the voice—

'Valentina,' Manolo acknowledged smoothly.

Of course, Valentina Vaquez. Singer, actress, occasional model. And a diva, Ariane remembered from

Tony's account of Valentina's behind-the-scenes tantrums during a video-taping session.

'You haven't answered any of my calls,' the actress chastised with a practised pout as she trailed perfectly manicured fingers over the lapel of his dinner suit. 'Very remiss of you, Manolo.' She cast a deliberate glance at Ariane and raised one perfectly shaped eyebrow. 'And you are?'

Oh, my, the actress displayed arrogance *plus*. 'Ariane.'

'My wife,' Manolo informed smoothly.

The announcement had a bombshell effect…as he no doubt meant it to.

'Really, darling?'

The actress recovered well, although perhaps it was only Ariane who caught the dangerous glitter apparent in those dark eyes before the expression was quickly masked.

Oh, my. Claws at dawn. Perhaps she should sharpen her own?

'Since when?'

'Yesterday.'

'No honeymoon?' She swept Ariane's slender frame a thinly disguised appraisal. 'How remiss of you not to insist on being whisked off to some exotic location.' The pause was deliberate. 'Or perhaps you're so thrilled to have him, you don't care?'

The *double entendre* didn't escape her, and she summoned a winsome smile. 'Should I answer that?'

Valentina pretended interest. 'I've seen you some-where—'

'Television,' Manolo revealed, carefully removing the actress's hand from his arm. An action which brought a slight moue of displeasure.

'Ah, yes, of course. Some sort of show...' Valentina trailed with derogatory uninterest.

The actress ran the manicured fingertip over the rim of her champagne flute, then cast Manolo a sultry look. 'If you'll excuse me? I really must mingle.'

With, unless Ariane was mistaken, the express intention of spreading a gossip coup.

'You could have warned me,' she issued quietly as soon as the actress was out of earshot.

'About Valentina?'

He was amused, and it rankled. 'Any more surprises I should prepare for?'

Manolo caught hold of her hand and lifted it to his lips. 'None of any consequence.'

His touch made her heart thud to a faster beat, heating the blood in her veins as she reacted to a base sexual chemistry. The memory of his lovemaking was hauntingly vivid, so much so she could *feel* him deep inside where stretched tissues still ached from his possession.

Did he know that? Sense it?

She'd slept curled against him for what remained of the night, and woken to the sound of Christina's early-morning cry echoing through the monitor. In one swift movement she'd slid from the bed, only to pause at her nakedness…when she never slept nude.

'Let's go in, shall we?'

Ariane heard Manolo's accented drawl, and registered the doors were open and the guests were moving into the ballroom.

If Valentina was seated at the same table, she'd scream. Surely fate couldn't be so unkind.

She should have known better. Not only did Valentina aim for their table, but she also slid into the seat directly opposite.

To accord it an interesting evening was an understatement. Although Ariane doubted *interesting* was the appropriate word.

The actress was clever, choosing to converse with most everyone at the table. Bright, scintillating conversation that seemed a mite overdone.

Was it only Ariane who picked up on the artificiality of Valentina's brilliant smile?

It was painfully obvious Valentina had Manolo in her sights, and unless she was mistaken the actress wasn't about to give up.

Had they been lovers? The thought made her feel ill.

Oh, for heaven's sake! What did it matter if they had?

Except the thought of Valentina's sinuous body wrapped around Manolo, indulging in skin-to-skin pleasure, bothered her far more than it should.

'More champagne?'

Ariane bore Manolo's scrutiny and offered a faint smile. 'Not at the moment.'

'You *are* attending Peter's opening night?' Valentina posed. 'Everyone is going.'

'I don't think so.'

The actress affected a delicate pout, Ariane silently acknowledged. The result of mirror practice?

'The art exhibition?'

Persistence ruled...but would Valentina win? Against Manolo? Not a chance! Unless he allowed it to happen.

Would he?

A camera flash provided a sudden burst of light, catching Ariane unawares, and was quickly followed by another.

'The newly married couple,' Valentina announced with a feline smile. 'Manolo and Ariane del Guardo.' She lifted her champagne flute and held it high in a silent toast Ariane doubted was meant to be congratulatory.

Were the fellow guests at their table aware of the subtle undercurrents? Probably not.

Word spread like wildfire, as the actress had intended it to. Tomorrow's newspapers would feature a photograph and a few lines. Ariane could picture it now. And Roger...he'd catch it, and react—*how*?

There were a few SMS text messages she should

send to a few close friends who would be hurt at not hearing the news first-hand.

The food looked delectable, and Ariane forked morsels without tasting a thing. The temptation to accept more champagne was irresistible, and she sipped it slowly, enjoying the light bubbles as they burst against her tongue.

'Something's been puzzling me,' Valentina broached with seeming innocence. 'Weren't you once married to Roger Enright? I seem to recall you garnered some media attention over a stalking incident not long after you separated.'

What was it with this woman? 'It was public knowledge at the time,' Ariane said quietly.

The actress feigned sympathy. 'It must have been hell.'

You have no idea.

'Does Roger know you've remarried?'

Was it her imagination, or had everyone at their table suddenly become silent?

'I prefer to keep my private life…private.' The slight emphasis was apparent.

'But surely you must be concerned there might be—' she paused for delicate effect '—repercussions?'

A restraining order was in force, but she'd lost count of the number of times Roger had broken it.

'You seem remarkably curious about something

which has no relevance in your life.' The words held a quiet warning Valentina chose to dismiss.

'Oh, but it does, sweetie. Manolo and I have been friends for years.'

Friends, huh? The term held several connotations. But he hadn't married the actress. Which had to say something.

'And you're merely expressing concern for his choice in me as a wife?' Two could play the game, and while she didn't care who won or lost, she refused to remain a passive contender.

'Good heavens.' Surprise, mild consternation, slight embarrassment. Valentina displayed each emotion well. 'Why should you think such a thing?'

Because that's what you meant to imply. 'Misinterpretation?'

'Most definitely.'

Ariane decided the jury was still out on that one.

Everyone at the table began to talk at once, and she spared a quick glance at Manolo, met and held his indolent gaze, caught the faint edge of amusement apparent, and clenched her fingers into a fist beneath her table napkin.

Within seconds he reached for her hand, worked her fingers apart and separated them with his own. An action which gave the opportunity to dig her nails in *hard*.

His only response was to stroke a thumb-pad over

the delicate veins at her wrist, which, if meant to soothe, didn't work.

There were speeches, which she listened to with apparent interest. Anything that fostered and benefited children, especially the sick and terminally ill, had her vote.

To anyone who chanced to look in her direction...and there were many who did...she determined to give every appearance of enjoying the evening.

'One can't imagine Manolo will agree to you continuing work,' Valentina posed during dessert, a course she dismissed with an elegant wave of her hand.

'There may be a special-interest project at some future time.'

'Such as Manolo's interest in deprived kids?' The actress effected a coy smile. 'Or perhaps you intend a little brood of your own?'

No matter how she qualified it, the barb stung.

'We have Christina.' Manolo's drawl held a silky quality Valentina chose to ignore.

'Of course.' The actress fixed Ariane with a calculating look. 'How convenient for Manolo to combine wife and live-in childminder in one package.'

'Yes, isn't it?'

Perfectly shaped eyebrows lifted a fraction as the actress shifted her attention to Manolo. 'We were together only a week ago, darling, and you made no mention then of a forthcoming marriage.'

Together could mean anything, Ariane allowed, so why was she leaping to the obvious conclusion?

'I see no reason to announce my plans.' Manolo's drawl held a slight edge that would have made a thinner-skinned person shrink into silence. 'To anyone.'

'You could have told *me*, darling.'

'No,' he reiterated smoothly.

'If you'll excuse me?' Valentina didn't wait to see if anyone objected. 'I'll go share coffee with Stefano.' With a practised flourish she stood to her feet and swept from the table.

'Lucky Stefano,' Ariane declared quietly, and incurred Manolo's wry smile.

'He chooses to handle her.'

'While you don't?'

'No.'

Should she be relieved? Don't be a fool, she chastised silently as the waiters began serving coffee to the tables.

Soft music provided a pleasant background, and guests began to move from table to table, catching up with friends.

'Shall we make a move to leave?'

Their passage through the ballroom was slow, given the number of people who, having heard of the marriage, deemed it necessary to offer a few congratulatory words.

Consequently it was almost eleven when Manolo brought the car to a halt inside the garage.

Home, Ariane declared silently. Except it didn't feel like *home*. Maybe it would, eventually.

Santos was in the nursery, reading, and Christina slept peacefully in her cot.

'She hasn't stirred,' Santos assured as he stepped out into the hallway. 'How was the evening?'

'Interesting.' Manolo's voice held a degree of cynicism.

'As in?'

'Valentina Vaquez,' Ariane elucidated, and saw Santos grimace.

'I see.'

'I'll leave Manolo to fill you in,' she said sweetly, and walked down the hallway to the master suite.

Within minutes she'd stripped off her clothes, added a robe, and was in the process of removing her make-up when she heard Manolo enter the room.

She took her time finishing up, then she unpinned her hair, and turned towards the door to see Manolo leaning against the door-jamb.

Black silk hipster briefs were all that saved him from total nudity, and she deliberately met his gaze.

'You don't owe me an explanation.'

'No.'

'Whatever Valentina was to you is none of my concern.'

'Agreed.'

She drew in a breath, then slowly released it. 'I would appreciate it if you'd let me know of any other women I might encounter who can lay claim to you, so I can be prepared.'

'Prepared to do…what?' he drawled lazily.

Amusement lurked in those dark eyes, and she reacted without thought, aiming a fist to his shoulder. Except a hand clamped her wrist before it reached its mark.

'Let me go.'

'Soon. First, we talk.'

'There's nothing to talk about.'

'Yes, there is. No thanks to Valentina, the media will run news of our marriage ahead of me making a formal announcement. How do you imagine Roger will react?'

'With anger.' It was just a matter of what form it would take.

'Santos will organise tightened security measures as from tomorrow. Meantime, I don't want you going anywhere alone.'

'I can look after myself.'

'Nevertheless, you won't chance it.' He lifted a hand and smoothed back a stray tendril of hair. 'Understood?'

How could she be angry, yet melt at his touch?

'Ariane?'

'Fine,' she capitulated. 'If you're done talking, I want to get some sleep. I'm tired.'

His hands settled on her shoulders. 'I can help with

that.' Was she aware how her eyes darkened when she became emotionally affected?

'Somehow I think your *help* involves me not sleeping for a while.' She didn't want to do this, told herself she wasn't in the mood…and knew she lied.

'Trust me.' His fingers lightly traced the edge of her jaw, then moved to outline her lower lip.

'Fatal,' she managed as she endeavoured to control the piercing sweetness consuming her body.

His hands skimmed her neck and slipped beneath the lapels of her robe. 'Want me to stop?'

She swayed a little as his head lowered to hers. 'Yes.' It was a brave effort that didn't fool either of them.

His mouth teased hers, and she sighed at her involuntary response. It felt good, so very good to be this close to him, and warmth surged to heat as he tantalised each tender peak, then trailed his mouth down to savour first one, then the other.

'Damn you,' Ariane whispered unsteadily when one hand slid over her stomach and settled low to linger and tease a little before seeking the swollen bud already throbbing in anticipation of his touch.

Her robe slid to the floor, quickly followed by his briefs, and she gasped as his fingers worked a wicked magic that sent her up and over, only to climb the heights of ecstasy again.

In one fluid move he grasped hold of her waist and lifted her high, then slowly slid her down his body, skin to skin, parted her thighs and wrapped her legs round his waist...then he sank into her.

Dear lord in heaven, Ariane breathed as he began to move. Tortuously slow at first, he increased the pace until it was all she could do to hold on.

Afterwards, curled up against him and on the edge of sleep, she brushed her mouth over one male nipple. 'I think I hate you.'

Her voice was an indistinct murmur, and Manolo smiled as he touched his lips to her hair. 'Go to sleep, *querida*. Whatever tomorrow brings, we'll face it together.'

Each of the Sunday newspapers carried a caption detailing news of Manolo del Guardo's marriage to Ariane Celeste, together with a photograph of each of them filched from an archive file.

It wasn't front-page, but sufficient attention was given to highlight the information and make it eminently noticeable.

Ariane kept her cellphone off, and waited until after breakfast when she was alone to check for messages.

The first came from a friend. Then Roger, over and over again spewing bitter invective.

She didn't see Manolo enter the room, nor did any sound alert her to his presence until he crossed to her side, removed the cellphone and held it to his ear.

'Por Dios.' The words emerged in husky remonstrance minutes later as he closed the unit. His eyes

speared hers. 'How long have you been receiving messages like these?'

'A while.'

His eyes hardened. 'Perhaps you'd care to define *a while*?'

'They began the day after I left him.'

There was no change in his expression, but something in his manner took on a dangerous undertone. 'How often does he message you?'

'Almost every day.'

'And they're this abusive?'

'It's a harassment campaign. In psychology-speak, he wants me to know he's aware of my whereabouts, what I do, who I see. I've changed unlisted numbers so many times I think I've broken any existing record.'

Manolo didn't query the existence of a restraining order. Mostly they were ineffective against an obsessive-compulsive personality.

'He uses different SIM cards, various land-lines so it becomes almost impossible to determine the caller's identity from the number displayed.'

'Leave it with me.'

'I doubt you can do anything I haven't done already.'

A statement that earned her a lifted eyebrow. 'Give your parents and Alex my private number for contact. Santos will arrange it for you and screen any incoming calls on your cellphone. Meanwhile, use the house land-line to make any necessary calls.'

It would take a miracle to get Roger's messages to cease.

'No, it won't,' Manolo assured with deceptive quietness. 'Trust me.'

He read minds? He seemed to have become adept at reading hers!

CHAPTER NINE

ARIANE spent the next few days organising things that had been left behind in the countdown to her wedding. There were the curiosity calls Santos fielded from some of Manolo's social contemporaries with invitations to one gathering or another…designed, she was sure, to discover more than the media and Manolo's formal announcement had revealed about their sudden marriage.

Invitations Santos duly noted and referred for Manolo's response.

'We're the flavour of the month,' Ariane alluded with wry humour over dinner Tuesday evening.

'Give it a few more days, and it'll be old news.' Manolo pushed his empty plate to one side and finished his wine.

'I had a call this morning from the production manager with a tentative date for when your documentary will go to air.' She retained a special interest in this one, for obvious reasons. 'He has it scheduled for next month.'

Manolo wondered if she realised how expressive her features were, and how easily he could read her. 'You did a good job of the interview.'

He watched the pleasure in her smile, the way it reflected in her eyes. 'Are you damning me with faint praise?'

His eyes gleamed with musing humour. 'What makes you think that?'

'I wanted more than you were prepared to give me,' she said quietly.

'Nitty-gritty, cut-to-the-bone stark realism?'

'I didn't want to whitewash the factual reality.'

He regarded her thoughtfully. 'There's only so much factual reality the viewing public can willingly handle. It would serve no purpose to emphasise the life I left behind.'

'Yet it's a part of who you are, what you've become because of it.'

'I can't change the yesterdays. I can only ensure I never return to them.'

'So you continue to build an empire.' His psyche intrigued her. 'How far do you go before it's far enough?'

'When it's no longer a challenge, when there's a shift in priorities.' He rose to his feet. 'Speaking of which, I have to go through some configurations on the computer before taking in a few meetings in Brisbane tomorrow.'

'How long will you be away?'

'Two days.'

She'd miss him. More than she was prepared to admit.

The days would be fine, but the nights?

Sex, she rationalised later that night as she lay in Manolo's arms on the edge of sleep.

Physical lust. Even thinking about what they shared together was enough to arouse sensual heat deep inside and have it flare through her body until every pleasure pulse ached with anticipatory need.

So she'd rent a few DVDs, write long emails to her parents, Alex, her friends. Develop an idea she'd entertained months ago for writing a series of articles.

Maybe, while Christina was asleep for her afternoon nap, she could ring Liesl on the off-chance she was off-duty and free to meet for coffee.

'Would you mind?' Ariane queried of Santos the next morning. 'Christina usually sleeps for three hours, and I'll only be away for two at the most. I'll take my cellphone, and if she wakes you must ring me at once.'

'Is Manolo aware of your plans?'

A musing smile teased her lips. 'Is he likely to object?'

'His concern is understandable.'

She sobered as his meaning hit home. 'I won't allow my everyday life to be affected by Roger's harassment.'

'Caution is advisable in this instance.'

'Since my remarriage?'

'To an exceedingly wealthy man,' Santos concluded.

'You imagine I haven't thought of that?' Examining each twist and turn should Roger decide to wreak revenge. 'I would never put Christina in jeopardy.' Her eyes darkened as she held his gaze. 'I can take care of myself,' she assured quietly.

Santos regarded her in silence for a few long seconds. 'You won't object if I call an hour after you leave to check you're OK?'

'Is that you talking, or Manolo?'

'Both. I take care of things in Manolo's absence.'

'And that includes me?'

'Does it bother you?'

She wasn't used to having her movements monitored. 'Yes.'

A faint smile curved his mouth. 'Honesty…an admirable quality.'

'I'm glad you agree.'

Ariane left a message on Liesl's voice-mail, then went upstairs to the nursery. Christina was beginning to stir, and Ariane watched as the babe woke, then felt her heart melt as the child's face smiled in recognition. Small legs pumped in excitement, and a chuckle emerged as she rolled over, then manoeuvred herself into an unsteady sitting position.

'Gorgeous,' Ariane accorded softly. 'Ready to play, sweetheart? First we do the nappy check, hmm?'

She really was a beautiful child, so bright and alert. Happy. Did she sense there was now some stability in her life? It would be nice to think so.

It was almost two when Christina settled for her afternoon nap, and Ariane quickly changed into cargo trousers, pulled on stiletto-heeled boots, added a trendy top, then went in search of Santos.

'I'm on my way.' She held up the new cellphone Manolo had insisted she have in lieu of her own. 'If you need me. Otherwise I'll be back around four.'

'I can easily help with Christina if she wakes before you return,' Maria declared.

Santos moved towards an electronic panel. 'I'll release the gates.'

It didn't take long for Ariane to reach Double Bay, and she was fortunate to gain a convenient parking space.

An exclusive suburb, its hub held numerous trendy boutiques and pavement cafés, small terrace houses built close together gutted and renovated into stylish shops where designer names flourished. Haute couture, she mused, imported from Italy, France and Germany.

People lingered over coffee, conversed, and enjoyed the process of being *seen*. But the atmosphere was something else, the coffee to die for.

'What took you so long?' a light feminine voice drawled, and a tall, svelte blonde folded her close in an enveloping hug.

'Liesl! I wasn't sure you'd be able to make it.' Ariane returned the hug, then drew back with a warm laugh. 'How are you?'

'Sit. And tell,' Liesl commanded as she summoned the young waiter and gave their order. 'In the name of all the saints...*Manolo del Guardo*.' Her voice was a reverent whisper. 'Girl, are you ever flying high. I want it all. *All*,' she warned. 'Like, how come you got married and didn't invite me? And why the rush and secrecy?'

Friends, the true kind, were rare. And Liesl was one of them. They'd met and bonded at boarding-school, and their friendship hadn't faltered in the years that followed.

'Caffeine first,' Ariane teased.

'Oh, no, you don't.'

'OK, I snagged an interview with Manolo,' she relayed simply. 'His daughter's nanny had just walked, I filled in a little, he asked me to stay on a few days. A week later he proposed.'

Sapphire-blue eyes narrowed in speculation. 'That's it?'

'More or less.'

'Sweetheart, there's a lot more to it than that. *Tell*.'

Ariane hesitated. 'It's an arrangement that suits us both.'

'*Arrangement*, huh? I've seen your gorgeous husband in the flesh, and he's to die for. So, who are you trying to kid?' She studied Ariane thoughtfully. 'Given your history, there are a few variables, but you wouldn't do *marriage* again unless you'd fallen for the guy.'

'You're wrong.'

'Am I?'

The waiter delivered their lattes, and Ariane broke a sugar tube, then stirred in the contents. 'Yes.'

'This is Liesl, remember,' the beautiful blonde said gently.

'It's not a love match.'

'Just…lust?'

Oh, yes, it was all of that! 'There's a beautiful baby whom I get to share and care for,' Ariane relayed quietly. 'A lovely home, a nice life.' She waited a beat. 'After Roger, I'm happy to settle for that.'

'If I didn't know you so well, I could almost believe you.'

Ariane sipped her coffee, then met her friend's gaze with solemn regard.

'And how is the infamous Roger taking all this?' Liesl pursued.

'Manolo is having my cellphone calls screened. Consequently I only get to receive the legitimate ones.' She paused in contemplative silence. 'It's to be hoped Roger will cease harassing me and move on.'

'Hmm. Like that's going to happen.'

She was very much afraid Liesl had it right. The calls would intensify in frequency…for how long, before he meticulously planned some form of revenge?

'Moving right along,' Liesl declared, 'what did you wear on *thé* day?' She offered an infectious grin. 'Do you have photos?'

'Santos took a few, one of which Manolo released to the media.'

'Santos is *who*?'

'Manservant, in charge of the household. He also cooks.'

'OK, so in lieu of photos, I want a detailed description.'

Ariane obliged, then sank back in her chair. 'Your turn. Fill me in on Emilio.'

Liesl effected a light shrug. 'He's in Milan. I'm here. What more can I say?'

'He adores you.'

'We're ships that pass in the night.'

'You could base yourself in Milan.'

'Maybe.'

A pensive response, if ever there was one. 'So what's the problem?'

'Ariane! Fancy seeing you here.'

Please, don't let it be Valentina Vaquez… Yet there she was, beautifully dressed and cosmetically perfect.

'Valentina,' she acknowledged, hoping the actress would move on.

She didn't. 'I thought you'd be home doing nanny duty.'

'Even nannies get to have some time off.'

'Liesl Vanhoffen,' Liesl extended with a practised smile. 'Ariane's friend.'

Did Valentina get the *mess with my friend, you mess with me* subliminal message? Doubtful!

The actress barely afforded Liesl a glance. 'I'm so glad I ran into you. Perhaps you can give me a few moments?'

What could she say? Don't answer that! 'Now isn't really convenient.'

Valentina merely lifted a dismissing hand. 'I'm hosting an auction of donated jewellery on Saturday evening to aid Manolo's charity. He will of course be the guest of honour. I don't expect you to attend.'

Liesl arched one eyebrow as Valentina swept away. 'Charming.'

'Isn't she?'

'Chocolate, or retail therapy?' Liesl queried wickedly.

'Why not both?'

Liesl tilted her head to one side. 'Retail therapy, definitely.' She extracted a note from her purse and tucked it beneath the saucer. 'My treat.' She stood to her feet. 'OK, my friend. Let's go flash some serious plastic.'

It was amazing what could be achieved in so short a time, Ariane concluded as she drove towards Point Piper an hour later.

There were no less than three glossy carrier bags resting on the rear seat, a testimony to Liesl's persuasive judgement on two *must-haves*. Ariane took total responsibility for the third.

Santos greeted her at the door.

'Any problems?' she queried as she entered the house.

'Christina hasn't stirred.'

But she would soon.

'I see you've had a successful time.'

Ariane lifted the carrier bags high, and proffered a mischievous smile. 'You could say that.'

'Manolo rang. He'll call after dinner. There are two messages from your screened calls. I've left details on the escritoire inside your suite.'

She felt compelled to ask. 'Roger?'

Santos' expression remained unchanged. 'Several, each duly recorded and erased.'

'I'm sorry.' Sorry he'd had to listen to such invective, repeated over and over again. There wasn't much else she could say without rehashing old history, the details of which he was already aware.

She indicated the bags. 'I'll take these upstairs, then check on Christina.'

It was almost eight by the time she'd settled the babe for the night, and she went down to the kitchen, took out the delectable salad Santos had prepared for her, then she sat down at the table.

'Would you like some tea?'

Santos was as silent on his feet as Manolo…a trait they shared.

'I can easily get it.' She cast him a steady glance. 'I'm not exactly helpless. And if you give me the excuse it's your job description to *serve*…forget it.'

'You're my employer's wife.'

'Lighten up.' She indicated the chair opposite. 'Why don't you take the weight off your feet, and be sociable for a while?'

'I'll make tea.'

Ariane looked at him carefully. 'Is this a supremacy thing? Your kitchen, your equipment?'

'Not at all.'

He made the tea, poured it into two cups and brought them to the table, then he pulled out a chair and sat down.

'You've known Manolo for some time.' Idle conversation, she mused, for her research into Manolo's background had revealed the friendship extended more than twenty years. Yet the ten-year gap in the two men's ages was intriguing.

'Yes.'

'It must have been difficult. No immediate family to rely on…'

'It wasn't easy.'

She looked at him thoughtfully. 'How did you meet each other?'

'A slight altercation developed into something nasty.'

'Who rescued whom?'

His eyes gleamed at the reflection. 'You could say it was a joint effort.'

'Ah, two against…?'

'A few.'

'I see.'

He doubted she did. *Tough* didn't begin to cover it. An ex-teen and an almost-teen, watching each other's back in circumstances no child should have to endure. Yet they'd survived, the bond remained, and when Manolo began travelling the road towards success he'd taken Santos with him. Something for which Santos was eternally grateful.

'Have you ever been back to the States?'

'No.'

At that moment the phone rang, and Santos rose to answer its summons, spoke for a few minutes, then held out the receiver. 'Manolo.'

Her stomach performed a series of somersaults as she crossed to take the call. 'Hi.'

'Ariane.' The sound of her name on his lips sounded impossibly sexy, and she clutched the receiver a little tighter as Santos removed himself from the room. 'How are you?'

'Fine.' Oh, for heaven's sake, get a grip. 'Christina is well.'

'So Santos informed me when I rang this afternoon.'

He probably also knew she'd been out for a few hours. 'I met Liesl for coffee.'

'A friend?'

'A very good friend,' she endorsed. 'How are things in the business arena?'

'Fairly straightforward. I'll be back tomorrow night.'

Was that amusement she caught in his voice? 'I thought you weren't due to return until Friday.'

'We should be able to wrap it up ahead of time.'

'Have fun,' she said lightly, and heard his faint chuckle ahead of her voiced 'goodnight'. She replaced the receiver before he had a chance to respond.

Ariane spent a restless night, rose early and managed an exhausting session in the gym, then, showered and dressed, she tended to Christina's needs, ate breakfast, and spent much of the day reorganising the nursery.

Dinner was a light meal, and afterwards she watched cable television for a few hours before ascending the stairs to bed.

It was almost eleven when she turned on the shower and stepped beneath the warm water-spray. Her muscles ached a little from her first work-out in almost a week, and she felt pleasantly tired.

She turned the dial up and luxuriated in the steamy heat as she picked up the soap and began lathering her skin.

Manolo hadn't called. Obviously he hadn't been able to wrap up the business deal ahead of time, and the wheeling and dealing would resume in the morning.

Ariane told herself she didn't care. She'd entered this marriage with her eyes wide open. There were going to be many lonely nights ahead of her as Manolo's business interests took him to several major capitals around the world.

Get used to it, she counselled silently, and slid the soap to a hard-to-reach spot between her shoulder blades.

'Let me help you with that.'

Ariane heard the masculine voice, had the soap removed from her hand simultaneously, and whirled round to face the very naked form of her husband. The hand she'd curled into a protective fist was caught before it could connect.

'You could have warned me!' Her eyes were dark green chips of spitting anger.

'And spoilt the surprise?'

'Dammit, you scared me half to death!'

Manolo's hands slid to her shoulders. 'Choose a tune and I'll whistle next time.'

The water had drowned out the sound of the shower door sliding open. Which didn't make it any easier to contain her nerves. 'I could have—'

'Wreaked an injury?' He was amused, and she could have killed him for it. 'Doubtful.'

'Give me back the soap.'

'Soon.' His head lowered down to hers, and she made a feeble attempt to avoid his seeking mouth. Without success, as his lips teased her temple, traced her cheekbone, then slid to her mouth in a sensuous assault.

She wanted to sink in against him and take…everything, she decided weakly as her bones began to liquify.

Heat fizzed through her veins, warming her body to fever pitch, and she groaned deep in her throat as his hands trailed a path to her ribcage, the curve of her waist, before sliding up to capture each breast. Teasing, tasting, suckling until she cried out at being held on the edge between pleasure and pain.

Manolo trailed his lips up her throat, then settled over her mouth in a kiss that rocked every part of her.

She was dying, soaring, completely mindless. *His*, unconditionally.

Almost as if he knew, he slid one hand low to seek and gift her pleasure, and she climbed high at his intimate touch, then he caught her cries as he took her over.

Again, and again. Then when she managed to catch her breath he reached for the soap and effected an evocative cleansing before placing the scented tablet in her hand.

'Your turn.'

Oh, my. His body was a muscular work of art, sculpted by nature's kind hand, sleek, smooth, *hard*. Everywhere.

She began with his shoulders and worked her way down. Way down. Carefully avoiding the most provocative part of his anatomy. Which wasn't very fair, given the pleasure he'd afforded her.

This man wasn't Roger. An all too vivid memory caused her hands to shake, and she quickly grasped his waist.

Not quickly enough. Manolo wrapped a hand beneath her chin and tilted it. 'In the name of heaven…' His eyes narrowed. When she didn't speak, he stifled a curse. 'Ariane?' His voice was silky, and dangerous with intent.

When she didn't answer, he traced a gentle path over her lower lip. 'He really did a number on you, didn't he?'

In spades.

Without a further word Manolo turned off the water, snagged a towel and wound it round his hips, then filched another and began to blot the moisture from her body.

She felt incredibly vulnerable, as if she'd disappointed him. It wasn't his fault, any more than it was hers. Maybe…

'Don't,' Manolo chastised gently. His lips brushed hers, fleetingly. He released her and rubbed the towel briskly over his torso, then he threaded his fingers through her own. 'Bed, hmm?'

She wanted to hold him, and be held. Close, so she could bury her cheek against the curve of his shoulder and breathe in the scent of his skin.

Stupid tears rose to the surface and shimmered, threatening to spill, and she blinked rapidly to dispel them as he led her into the bedroom.

A touch on the electronic module and the lights dimmed low. Seconds later he pulled her down onto the bed and into his arms.

'I missed you.' His mouth brushed her cheek and slid down to the edge of her mouth. 'This.' He kissed her gently at first, then took her deep, absorbed her sigh, and began a tantalising exploration that led to an erotic tasting so exquisite she begged his possession.

Something he gave with a passion she matched, exulting in the joy of good sex.

Very good sex, she accorded dreamily as she curled into him and hovered on the edge of sleep.

It was during breakfast next morning when she was reaching for her second coffee refill that she suddenly remembered Valentina's message.

'I forgot to tell you I ran into Valentina yesterday.'

Manolo's eyes sharpened as he regarded her over the breakfast table. 'Indeed?'

'She walked by the café where Liesl and I were sharing coffee,' she explained. 'Valentina asked me to remind you about the jewellery auction she's holding on Saturday evening.'

Something for which Valentina had instigated arrangements two months ago. Invitations had already been sent, interest expressed...

'Apparently you haven't returned her calls.'

'I have a director in charge of fund-raising activities,' Manolo relayed. 'Valentina has his name and contact number.'

'She prefers, however, to make it a personal issue?'

The woman was unshakeable. 'Yes.'

'I see.'

He leaned back in his chair and surveyed her solemnly. 'Do you?'

'You want *polite*?'

'Be frank, by all means.'

Was that a glimmer of a smile at the edge of his lips? 'Valentina has a *thing* for you.'

'Don't stop now.'

Well, he asked for it. 'She refuses to let go.'

'And?' he queried silkily, and she went for honesty.

'I'm considered expendable.'

His eyes narrowed. 'She said as much?'

'She didn't need to.'

'Since I have no intention of attending any social function without you, Valentina is bound for disappointment.'

'Christina—'

'Santos will manage admirably for the few hours we'll be away.'

Ariane's eyes assumed a wicked sparkle. 'I could play the part of devoted wife.' Without any effort at all.

His soft laughter almost undid her. 'Into battle, huh?'

'Watch me.'

CHAPTER TEN

DRESSED TO KILL took on a connotation all its own as Ariane put the finishing touches to her make-up, then added antique earrings.

The gown she'd chosen for tonight's soirée was a signature Saab in ultra-feminine silk and chiffon featuring a halter-neck, a thigh-high split, with delicate embroidery and beading. The pastel eau-de-Nil complemented the creamy texture of her skin, brought out the colour of her eyes, and she wore her hair loose.

Stiletto-heeled pumps, matching evening bag, and she was ready.

'Sensational,' Manolo murmured appreciatively as he fixed his tie, then he reached for his jacket.

'Hmm.' She examined him from head to toe in a studied appraisal. 'You'll pass.'

'Just *pass*, huh?'

His musing query did strange things to her equilibrium. 'How could you miss?' she responded lightly. 'Fine Italian tailoring, handstitched shoes…' The pause was deliberate. 'Of course, the man wearing them has a certain…something.'

The edges of his mouth twitched. 'Really?'

Her chin lifted a little, and her eyes held a mischievous sparkle. 'I take it we're ready to go play?'

'Remind me to deal with you later.'

'Interesting.'

'It will be.'

They stopped at the nursery to check on Christina, who was sleeping peacefully. Serenity in a child was an awesome quality, and Ariane's heart seemed to execute a tiny flip at the degree of affection, the fierce maternal connection she had for Manolo's daughter.

Except Christina was also Yvonne's child, and she had the instinctive urge to discover more about the woman Manolo had married.

There were no framed photographs in evidence anywhere in the house. Not even a wedding photo. She wasn't mentioned, and it was almost as if she'd never existed.

It wasn't a query she felt inclined to ask...at least, not here, not now.

Don't sweat the small stuff, she warned silently. Except the woman who'd borne his child didn't fall into the *small stuff* category.

It would be nice to think she was making a difference, Ariane reflected wistfully. To the child, without doubt. But what of Christina's father?

Was there any hope things would change and love might grow? On her part, it was almost a given. But on his?

What if he tired of her after a few months...a year,

and sought the bed of another woman? How would she cope with that?

A chill shiver slid down her spine. Not easily. Not easily at all.

She tried to tell herself it didn't matter. But it did. Very much.

A hand touched her waist, and she turned towards Manolo, aware of the need to leave. His expression was impossible to fathom, and she didn't even try.

Valentina's apartment was situated in exclusive Rose Bay, and had magnificent views over the harbour. Invitation only ensured the cream of Sydney's wealthy élite were present. Security measures were strict, identification thorough, and Ariane was intrigued by the effort Valentina had put into tonight's soirée.

For the benefit of Manolo's charity…or to impress Manolo, the man?

Be nice, she scolded silently. The charity would certainly benefit. And Manolo?

Valentina had obviously tried to move on him, without success. So why didn't that reassure her?

'Darling, there you are!'

The actress looked stunning in a black backless halter-neck gown slashed to the waist, displaying an extremely generous *décolletage*.

Perfection, Ariane accorded silently, and rather wickedly wondered if and when someone would announce *lights, camera, action*.

'Valentina,' Manolo acknowledged with a seem-ingly warm smile. He didn't like being manipulated, and wouldn't have allowed it, had Valentina not clev-erly nominated the evening's proceeds to aid his char-ity.

'You brought Ariane. How sweet.'

Sweet? Ariane indulged in the air-kiss routine, and reminded herself she was merely playing a part.

Drinks, canapés, uniformed waiters…everything appeared perfectly staged for the main players of the evening. And as if there was any doubt, Valentina soon made it very clear that, while Manolo was the star, *she* was hostess.

Ariane wandered towards the exhibits elegantly displayed on royal-blue velvet in a locked glass cab-inet. Each item bore a number, and each guest had been handed a printed programme summarising the history of each piece, its origin.

A pair of graduated emerald drop earrings caught her eye. Each emerald integrated with a small dia-mond. They were incredibly beautiful, and she failed to understand how their owner could bear to part with them.

'See anything you like?'

She turned at the sound of that familiar drawling voice, and felt her nerve-ends begin to fizz at the sight of the man who stood at her side.

'Am I supposed to clutch your arm, whisper seductive promises in your ear, then indicate the most expensive item in the cabinet?'

Manolo's eyes gleamed with amusement. 'Something like that.'

'Is it expected?'

'Seductive promises?'

Ariane silently damned the heat flaring through her body. 'I don't possess a particularly inventive repertoire.'

He lifted a hand to her nape, lingered there, then trailed a path to the edge of her waist. 'I have no complaints.'

'Ah, Manolo,' she gently mocked. 'A compliment?'

Did she have any idea how warm and generous she was in his arms? Or how delightful it was to feel her body quiver beneath his touch? The taste of her? To know her response was genuine, and not the result of clever faking? Or that he wouldn't know the difference?

'Perhaps we should focus on the jewellery,' he opined with indolent amusement. 'The auction is about to begin.'

'And Valentina is about to claim your attention,' Ariane murmured with edged cynicism as the actress closed in on them.

'Manolo.'

The actress's smile held a seductive sorcery...the

curve of her lips, the teasingly provocative gleam in those knowing eyes.

Talk about eating a man alive!

'I need to steal you for a while.'

The implication was subtle, and Ariane offered a musing smile. 'Go have fun, *querido*,' she bade lightly. 'Just remember I get to take you home.'

He took hold of her hand and lifted it to his lips. 'As if I could forget.'

The soft drawl held a seducing quality that shattered her composure and set all her nerve-ends on pulsing alert.

Dear heaven, he was good! If he continued in this vein, he'd be in danger of serious overkill.

Ariane caught the venomous gleam evident in Valentina's eyes before it was quickly masked, and felt a chill slide over her skin.

It was almost an anticlimax as the official part of the evening began, with a charming introduction by the actress. Manolo outlined the purpose of his charity, thanked Valentina for organising the event, then handed over to the auctioneer.

The bidding was spirited, and two hours later every piece had been sold. Valentina positively glowed as she basked in the resultant success.

Coffee and tea were served, and Ariane mixed and mingled as Manolo was caught…*trapped*, she amended, by a few guests headed by Valentina, who seemed bent on defining her position at his side.

'You present a show on television.'

Ariane turned towards the man who'd chosen to join her, and offered a polite smile.

'Don't tell me.'

It was almost possible to see the memory cogs clicking in motion. Suave, sophisticated…and delivering a practised line.

'Got it…intimate portraits of the rich and famous.'

Charm was part of her job description, and she did it well. 'Thank you.'

'Can I get you more coffee? A drink?' His pause was fractional, and deliberate. 'Anything?'

He was attractive, polished, and way too smooth. She aimed for polite regret. 'No.'

'You're here with someone?'

She inclined her head. 'My husband.'

He slipped a card into her hand. 'Give me a call, and we'll get together.'

Not in this lifetime. 'Thanks, but no, thanks.'

'You don't know who I am?'

She managed to keep the smile in place. 'Why don't you go hit on someone else?'

'Now I'm intrigued. Your husband is…?'

Ariane waited a few seconds, delaying the moment. 'Manolo del Guardo.'

'Hell.' The word slipped out unbidden, but he recovered well. 'We were just discussing—'

'The auction?'

'The auction,' he agreed. 'I think I'll get a coffee refill.'

Amusement teased the edges of her mouth as he beat a hasty retreat.

'It would seem you've crushed one male ego,' Manolo drawled minutes later.

'I mentioned your name.'

He lifted a hand and tucked a stray tendril of hair behind her ear. 'Indeed?'

'It had a remarkable effect.'

He was close, much too close. Worse, she suddenly became conscious of her breathing, the way her pulse seemed to jump to a throbbing beat.

What was happening here? Any second soon she'd lose what composure she had left. It was crazy, insane...*magic*.

Oh, dear God, she whispered silently. She couldn't be falling for him. Affection, respect, sex...she could deal with. But *love* was something else, and a one-sided love was a recipe for disaster.

You're wrong, you *have* to be wrong, she reiterated as she attempted to bring her body under control. Love doesn't happen as quickly as this.

Says who? a mischievous imp taunted.

'The auction went off very well.' The words fell from her lips in too much of a hurry, and she silently damned them.

'Yes.' He brushed light fingers down her cheek. 'We'll leave soon.'

Sensation unfurled deep inside, and raced through her body at the seductive quality in his voice, leaving her in no doubt how he intended the evening to end.

At that moment Ariane caught sight of Valentina moving towards them, and wondered at the actress's intention.

'Am I interrupting something?' The smile didn't reach her eyes. 'Manolo, one of the guests wants to speak with you.' She named him, waited until Manolo excused himself, then aimed for the kill.

'We need to talk.'

Here it comes…the move Ariane had been expecting all evening. 'I can't imagine we have anything to discuss.'

'Darling, don't play dumb. Manolo, of course.'

Surprise, surprise. How could it be anything else?

'Then I suggest you take it up with him,' Ariane said quietly.

'I can't think what you do that I—'

'Can't do better?' she posed, and saw the actress's mouth compress.

Valentina's dark eyes glittered with suppressed anger. 'It won't last. I was there before Yvonne, before *you*. He'll be mine again.'

This had gone far enough. 'Don't you think it's time to quit?'

For a moment she thought the actress was going to strike her. There was so much pent-up emotion, such dark rage apparent before she brought it under control.

'Watch your back.'

'Always.'

Manolo's return wrought a miraculous personality change in one second flat.

'Darling, I was just telling Ariane we should celebrate the evening's success.'

'You've been extremely generous in hosting tonight's event.' He'd ensure she was compensated. 'Another time, perhaps?' He offered a friendly smile. 'We have to consider the babysitter.'

Ariane had to admire the practised ease with which he extricated himself. It was an acquired panache that wasn't lost on Valentina, for she subsided with an elegant lift of her slim shoulders.

'Of course.'

It was late when Manolo brought the car to a halt in the garage. Santos greeted them at the head of the stairs, imparted Christina hadn't stirred, bade them 'goodnight', and retired to his quarters.

It took only minutes to check Christina before entering the master suite.

Ariane removed her earrings, then slid off her stilettos, aware Manolo had loosened his tie and was in the process of shrugging out of his jacket.

'I have something for you.' He reached a hand into the inside jacket pocket and extracted a small flat velvet box.

She was intent on undoing the fastening of her gown, and her fingers stilled as he crossed to where she stood.

'I didn't see you bid.'

'I had someone do it for me.'

'You shouldn't have' seemed clichéd and ungracious, so she didn't utter the words as he placed the velvet box in her hand.

'Open it.'

His thought to gift her anything was more important than the gift itself, and her lips parted in surprised pleasure at the emerald and diamond drop earrings nestled against their velvet background.

She stroked a finger over one drop, then met his gaze. 'They're beautiful.'

'They match your eyes.' His mouth curved with musing humour, watching the soft colour creep over her cheekbones. Did she realise how well he could read her emotions? The light, teasing sparkle when something amused her? The acquired depth when she was disturbed or reflective? Or the darkest emerald when caught up in the throes of passion?

'Thank you.'

His soft laughter almost undid her as his hands shaped her face. 'My pleasure, *mi mujer*.' He undid the halter-neck fastening, then slid the zip free, before easing the silk and chiffon from her body.

A delicate silk thong was all that saved her from total nudity, and she swayed slightly as he lowered his head to close his mouth over hers in a kiss that teased a little with the promise of what they would soon share.

He took it slow, so slow she was burning up, and she reached feverishly for the buttons on his shirt, slipped them free and sighed when she touched the smooth texture of his skin.

She loved the feel of him, the strong muscle and sinew, the scent and taste of him. Pheromones, *his*, were a powerful aphrodisiac, and she wanted more, so much more.

What would it take to have him lose control? Totally, over the edge…beyond reason?

Dared she even *try* to go there?

He was wearing too many clothes, and she was hardly aware of unfastening his trousers or accepting his help.

Dear heaven, he felt so good. So alive, so incredibly sexual as he pulled her in close.

His mouth, his hands…he had the touch, the sensual knowledge to drive a woman wild.

In his arms she lost all sense of time and place as she became enmeshed in emotions so intense she thought she might shatter into myriad splintering shards. Electrifying passion at its zenith, incandescent, it liquified her bones and made her *his*…body and soul.

There was a sense of tumultuous wonder in that *this* was how lovemaking was supposed to be. A generous gift of shared sensual pleasure…not the selfish taking by one participant without consideration or care for the other. No post-coital post-mortem filled with accusation and blame.

To love and be loved in return would be the ultimate, she reflected hazily as she lay sensually sated and replete in the drifting afterglow of very good sex.

To have it *all*. Was it too much to hope for?

Go with the now, a silent sage offered. Enjoy each day, each night without redress.

CHAPTER ELEVEN

SELF-COUNSELLING was a fine thing, Ariane reflected as the following days merged into a week.

Days when she helped Maria while Christina napped. She also took an interest in Santos' culinary expertise as they conferred on dishes, experimented a little with recipes.

There was time devoted to a daily work-out, an interesting project she was compiling on her laptop from a sheaf of notes.

Manolo spent most waking hours wheeling and dealing, leaving early each weekday for his city office, and as each day progressed there was the excitement, the anticipation of what each night would bring.

In his arms, she became someone she had never imagined she could ever be…so caught up in him, so much a part of him, it was as if their souls merged and became one.

Did he experience the same degree of emotional intensity? Sexual enjoyment and fulfilment, without doubt.

Unconditional love was the ultimate gift. Was it too much to hope for that *love* might combine with passion? Or was she merely being a sentimental fool?

Life, Ariane reflected, was good. And if love didn't enter Manolo's equation…well, she could handle it.

The only blip on the horizon was Roger, whose voice and text messages had intensified since her marriage and move into Manolo's home.

Granted, she no longer dealt with them on an ongoing basis. However, it was difficult to dampen her concern as to how, if, or when Roger's delusional behaviour might manifest itself into more than harassment.

Santos continued to screen the calls to her cellphone, and referred only the genuine messages.

One of which was a reminder confirming her commitment to *compère* a fashion show scheduled for Tuesday at one of the inner-city hotels.

'I meant to call the committee president and cancel,' she explained as she slid into bed. 'But with one thing and another…' Her marriage to Manolo being one of them.

'Maria and Santos can manage Christina for a few hours,' Manolo drawled as he drew her in close. 'There's no reason why you shouldn't combine full-time motherhood with outside interests.' His lips trailed down to the edge of her mouth. 'Now, if you're done talking, I have something much more interesting in mind.' He teased the tip of his tongue along her lower lip. 'Like making love to my wife.' He dipped into her mouth, savoured a little, then trailed a path down the sensitive curve of her throat.

'Whose beautiful body I'll have to do without for the next seven nights.'

'While you tie up deals and wine and dine in New York.' It was fun to tease a little, to let go without being constantly on edge awaiting the belittlement Roger had subjected her to. 'Some hardship.'

The edges of his teeth grazed her breast, and he feasted there, then slid low, sensed her reaction and settled in for a long, slow loving that brought her alive…a willing wanton who never ceased to delight him with her response.

He would miss her. Miss having her warm body curled close to his throughout the night. She was a generous lover, gifting herself without condition or calculated performance.

Was it possible she was beginning to get beneath his skin? No woman had succeeded in reaching the heart of him.

Twice he reached for her through the night, and again just as the dawn began to finger a grey light through the darkness. Then he rose, showered, dressed, caught up his bag, briefcase and laptop, and took the car to the airport.

Two days later Ariane took the microphone at one of the prestigious fashion shows of the season.

The venue was well-patronised…a sell-out, the committee president informed. Lunch was part of the deal, and the fashion show kicked off when the guests had finished the main course.

Funky music, beautiful models, great fashions.

One thing she could have done without was the discovery Valentina Vaquez was one of the participating models.

So, don't let it get to you, she admonished silently. Just get into *compère* mode, and follow the programme.

It went well. The models performed, and so did she, injecting verve and vivacity for the benefit of the guests. *Image*, she reminded, was everything.

At the end of the show, she was thanked and presented with a floral bouquet, then it was time to leave.

'Ariane.'

Any hope of escaping without running into Valentina was lost as she turned towards the actress moonlighting as model for the day. 'Valentina.'

'I didn't think you'd show.'

And I was hoping *you* wouldn't! She aimed for polite. 'Why would you think that?'

The actress deliberately widened her eyes. 'Aren't you supposed to be chained to the child?' She took time to examine faultlessly lacquered nails before lancing Ariane's gaze. 'That *is* why Manolo married you?'

Without missing a beat Ariane picked up on the hidden challenge. 'Let's not forget the regular sex.'

'Oh, darling, don't imagine you're anything special. Women fall over themselves to perform for him.'

'Including you?'

Valentina excelled herself with melting, misty-eyed reflection. 'He's a lusty beast.'

'Yes,' Ariane agreed with a serenity she was far from feeling. 'Isn't he?'

'I wonder if Manolo has everything on your infamous ex.'

'What's to know,' anger began to unfurl and build, 'that wasn't made much of by the media at the time?'

'I hear he rings you every day. Even now.'

You don't have to justify anything, she reminded silently. 'Let it go, Valentina.'

'It must be hell for you.'

Pseudo-sympathy she could do without. 'Is there a point to this conversation?'

'Just to let you know I'll be waiting for you to fall from grace. As you will.'

'So you can pick up the pieces?'

The lacquered nails seemed to require Valentina's further inspection. 'I can play *mother*, too, darling. Remember that.'

Over my dead body! The thought of Christina in the actress's care made her feel physically ill. 'If you play the part so well,' she said carefully, 'one has to wonder why Manolo didn't put a ring on your finger, instead of mine.'

As an exit line it was perfection. Ariane turned and

didn't look back as she made her way to the foyer and had the porter organise to call up her car.

'Is there anything you need from the supermarket?' Santos enquired as Ariane rinsed her plate and stacked it into the dishwasher after breakfast the next morning.

'Thanks, no. I picked up a few things on the way home yesterday.' And took time out for a latte, in order to recoup her composure following her clash with Valentina!

'Maria will be a little late, and the gardener is due soon.'

'Check,' Ariane concurred as she sipped the last of her coffee. 'I'll go give Christina her bath, then settle her down for her morning nap.'

Ariane enjoyed the daily routine. Christina's morning naps were becoming short. She was an active, alert babe who adored the stimulating educational games they played together. And bath-time was a fun exercise all of its own.

It was almost ten-thirty when she put the babe down for her nap, and she collected the monitor remote and ran lightly down the stairs.

She could hear the faint buzz of the lawnmower in the background, indicating the gardener's arrival, and Maria was busy polishing furniture in the foyer.

The phone pealed, and Maria pulled the hand-held

unit from her pocket, intoned a customary greeting, then lapsed into a flood of her own language.

'Is everything OK?' Stupid question when Maria was so obviously upset.

'It's the school office. My daughter has broken her arm, she's being taken to the hospital—'

Ariane made an instant decision. 'You have to go. Take the rest of the day off. Manolo is away, everything here is fine.'

'You sure?' Maria looked doubtful. 'Santos is not here.'

'But he will be soon,' she reassured. 'Now go. Your daughter needs you.'

'Maybe I should wait until Santos gets back.'

'Are we going to stand here and argue?'

'No, no argument.' She removed her apron, collected her holdall, then exited the front door as Ariane released the gates.

Slight change in routine. She'd finish the polishing for Maria instead of doing a work-out, then she'd organise something for lunch.

The buzz of the intercom came as a surprise, and she crossed to the video surveillance screen, pressed the audio button requesting identification, saw a card against a background mass of flowers, and heard a voice relay, 'Delivery of flowers for Ariane del Guardo.'

Manolo had sent her flowers?

She released the gates. 'You can drive up to the front door.'

At that moment the phone rang and she collected the hand-held unit.

'Santos. I'll be delayed half an hour.'

'No problem.' There seemed no point in explaining Maria's absence as the doorbell sounded, and she hurried towards the door.

Ariane registered the mass of flowers as soon as she opened the door. They completely obscured the delivery guy's features, and premonition hit a mere second ahead of him shoving her indoors.

Two things happened simultaneously. The flowers hit the floor and the door shut.

Roger.

Calm; dear heaven, she had to remain calm. 'If you turn around and leave, I won't report this to the legal authorities.'

How could she ever have thought she cared for this man? Because he was a good actor...the best, she reminded. So good, he'd even fooled her and every one of her family, her friends. For months.

He was leaner than she remembered, and his eyes held a hardness that bordered on cruelty.

'So this is where you live.' He let his gaze rove around the foyer, noting the marble floors, the chandelier, the sweeping double staircase. 'Hit the jackpot, haven't you?'

Santos would be back in half an hour. Maybe sooner.

The gardener...maybe he'd become suspicious of a florist's delivery van standing at the main entrance longer than it should. *If* the gardener had even seen the van arrive.

There was the hand-held phone. Santos' cellphone was on auto-dial. If she could activate the connection and press the correct number...

It was worth a try, if she could manage to distract Roger long enough. The major problem was the electronic beep accompanying each touch-pad.

'Is he good?'

Ariane felt her stomach sink. She knew where this was leading. Even so, she sought to stall him. 'Who?'

'Don't play dumb.'

Think. Don't say anything he can misconstrue or use in accusatory anger. 'He's kind.'

Roger's mouth curved into a lopsided smile. *'Kind.'* He examined the word, rolled it around his tongue, then spat it out. 'He'll soon tire of you.'

Focus, concentrate on the phone's number configuration. *On, auto-dial,* numerical *two*.

Sick, remember he's sick. Just talk, keep talking.

'I'll deal with it, if and when he does.'

Pray, she bade silently. Pray Christina doesn't wake. Pray she doesn't cry.

'You should have answered my calls.'

She calculated where she could kick to put him on the floor…and how to achieve maximum impact.

'To do so would have contravened the restraining order.'

'All I wanted to do was talk to you.'

That was why he left lewd voice messages, and continued a harassment campaign? 'You've conspired this opportunity,' she ventured carefully as she fingered the phone's touch-pad. *On.* 'Why not use it?' *Auto-dial.* 'I'm listening.' Numerical *two.* 'Go ahead.'

Oh, dear heaven, had he registered the beeps?

'Won't do you any good, darling. Your husband's manservant has two flat tyres, courtesy of *moi.*' His eyes held an evil glitter. 'He's not going to come to your rescue any time soon.'

There was just one thing Roger had no hope of knowing. Her call to Santos' cellphone had copied to the security firm who would in turn immediately notify the police.

How long did she have? Five minutes? Ten?

Act scared. He fed on fear. 'It was worth a try.'

'Clever little thing, aren't you?' He moved forward a pace, and laughed as she stepped back. 'Never could understand the brilliance of my dual personality.' He began to circle her.

'I had fun with you. The courtship. Oh, you were so *sweet.* So trusting, so affectionate.' He thrust his hands into the back pockets of his jeans.

'It almost made me sick.' He turned his head and

spat on the floor. 'And so virginal. You had to be a *saving myself for the right guy* sort of girl, didn't you?'

He circled her again, watching her as she turned with him. 'You couldn't turn a trick if you tried. Wanted to have a child. Couldn't do that, either, could you?'

He was getting wound up, his voice lowering to a guttural snarl. Any minute soon he'd emphasise his frustration with a physical move.

'I taught you good, didn't I? Hurt you if you wouldn't perform.' He moved suddenly, and laughed at her reaction. 'A few slaps never hurt a woman. Keeps 'em in line.'

His eyes darkened, and she went incredibly still. 'Maybe I should slap you around a little now. Make you see sense.'

'Don't.' A warning he refused to heed.

'You shouldn't have left.' He jabbed her arm with a hard forefinger. 'I married you. For better or worse. You should have stayed. Why didn't you stay?'

She didn't answer, and he pushed her...*hard*. Hard enough she had to struggle to maintain her balance.

'All that stuff about the police, lawyers. Divorce. Why did you do that?'

The gates. Had she pressed the module to close the gates? If she had, no one would be able to get in. Then rationale made itself felt. A delivery van would deliver and leave within minutes. She'd have left the gates open.

A fist crashed into her ribs…swift, unexpected, and although she moved to deflect it, he managed to connect.

Work-outs, combative training enabled automatic reaction as she aimed a body kick with startling accuracy.

Roger fell to the floor, temporarily winded, and she trapped him there with her foot on his windpipe.

She was beyond pain as she extracted the hand-held phone, and redid the auto-dial.

Santos answered on the first ring. 'Ten seconds. You OK?'

'He's…' Oh, hell, what did they say in this sort of situation? '…secure.'

'We're in the driveway.' She heard the squeal of hastily applied brakes. 'At the door.'

Then they were there. Santos, the police, ambulance.

'*Ambulance?*' Ariane queried incredulously, and met Santos' grim expression.

'A necessary precaution.'

A sequence of events occurred simultaneously with Roger handcuffed and escorted into a police car while the paramedics checked her over, pronounced her rib-cage severely bruised, confirmed no ribs broken, suggested X-rays as a precaution, filled in a radiography slip, and appeared dubious when she refused to be taken to hospital.

'I'll see to it,' Santos assured firmly…a dictum she viewed with disfavour minutes ahead of being interviewed by the police.

It was around then the baby monitor emitted sounds of Christina stirring, and Ariane looked at the officer taking notes.

'Are you done? I need to go check my daughter.' Christina. She'd meant to say *Christina*. Just went to show what slip-ups could occur under stress.

'That's most of it,' the officer concurred. 'We'll get back to you when we've reviewed the phone tape.'

'Ariane—'

'I'm fine,' she assured Santos, who appeared unconvinced, and she ignored any further protest by heading upstairs to the nursery.

Santos joined her there soon afterwards, where he took one look at her pale features and moved to take Christina from her arms.

'Please. I'm fine. Really.' She even managed a faint smile. 'It could have been worse.'

'I've contacted Manolo.'

Ariane closed her eyes, then opened them again. All hell would break loose. 'It could have waited until his return.'

'No,' Santos refuted. 'It couldn't.'

She didn't want to think about his reaction. 'I'll

call him.' Tell him first-hand Christina was fine, *she* was fine.

Santos checked his watch. 'He'll be airborne very soon.'

'He's coming back?' she queried, aghast.

'Of course. Did you imagine he wouldn't?'

'But he has meetings—'

'None of which hold importance over your welfare.'

Ariane shook her head. 'That's crazy.'

'You think so?'

She wasn't up for cryptic conversations, and as if in silent agreement Christina began rocking back and forth and pushed a small fist to her mouth.

'She needs her lunch.' She stood to her feet and tried not to wince at the pain caused by the movement.

'Let me tend to her, then we'll go get those X-rays done.'

Ariane threw him an exasperated look. 'If you don't stop treating me like a fragile flower, I'll scream.'

Was that a glimmer of admiration, or just her imagination? 'Please.' She tried for calm. 'If you must do something, I'd love one of your chicken salad sandwiches for lunch and something long and cool to drink.'

He stood his ground. 'Perhaps—'

'You want me to heap feminine temperament on

your head?' she demanded fiercely, and saw his mouth twitch.

'Heaven forbid. Lunch first, then the hospital.'

The resultant diagnosis was three fractured ribs and severe bruising. Strong painkillers were prescribed, and Santos collected them.

Christina was content in her baby capsule, her eyes brightly observant as she took in all the sights and sounds so vastly different from the tranquillity of her nursery.

'You should rest,' Santos declared when they re-entered the house.

'I'll get an early night. Promise,' Ariane added as she took the babe upstairs for her afternoon nap.

It took longer than usual to settle Christina for the night, and Ariane sought distraction with a good novel, only to discard it and channel-hop between television programmes before giving up and going to bed.

On impulse she filled the spa-bath and sank into its heated depths.

Bliss, she accorded, closing her eyes.

She must have slipped into a light doze, that hazy place between wakefulness and sleep when the senses were not quite fully alert and there was little sense of time or place.

The faint click of the *en suite* door opening brought her sharply awake, and her eyes widened measurably as Manolo closed the door behind him, then slowly began removing his clothes.

'What do you think you're doing?'

Was that her voice? It sounded impossibly husky.

'Joining you.'

She watched in mesmerised fascination as he shed his shirt, his trousers, then he skimmed off his briefs before stepping in to sink down at her side.

There were words she wanted to say, to explain, and her lips parted, only to have a finger press against them.

'Shut up,' Manolo bade gently, as he leaned towards her and lowered his mouth close to hers. 'Just—' his lips brushed hers, lingered, then lifted fractionally '—shut up,' he reiterated softly a second before his mouth possessed hers in a kiss that was so incredibly gentle her eyes shimmered with unshed tears.

It seemed a while before he lifted his mouth from hers, and she looked into those dark eyes so close to her own and almost drowned.

'Christina is fine,' she managed, hating that her voice shook a little.

'And you, *querida*?' Did she have any conception what he'd been through? Santos' phone call…being so far away and having to wait all these hours to reach her? Listening to Roger's invective? Aware how much worse it could have been? He'd gone from icy anger to burning rage just thinking about it.

To say it should never have happened was fruitless. Roger had bided his time, taken note of Manolo's household routine, and circumstance had aided his plan with the bonus of Maria's absence, leaving Ariane alone in the house.

What could she say? Roger had skated so close to the line and crossed it numerous times. Now he had to pay. 'Relieved,' she said quietly. 'He needs help. Maybe now he'll get it.'

Manolo closed his eyes momentarily. He'd already engaged a team of top lawyers. Roger Enright didn't stand a chance in hell of experiencing freedom in a long time.

As to security measures…how much was enough before it bordered on overkill?

One thing for sure…he'd do whatever it took to ensure nothing like this ever happened again.

There were words he wanted to say. And he would…soon. For now, he needed to fold her close in against him, breathe in the clean, fresh smell of her hair, her skin.

With care he stepped out of the tub, snagged a towel, and dried the excess moisture from his body before fastening the towel on one hip. Then he lifted her out and gently blotted her dry.

'Don't,' Ariane murmured as he traced the reddened swelling beneath her left breast.

His eyes darkened until they were almost black, and his mouth tightened into an ominous line.

'Please.' She couldn't bear his silent anger. 'It's done.'

'Bed, hmm?' Manolo murmured gently, and brushed his lips to her temple. 'It's been a long day for both of us.'

He led her into the bedroom, slid back the covers and watched her slip beneath them, then he slid in beside her.

Without a word he pulled her in against him and buried his mouth in the sweet curve of her neck. One hand slid to cup her buttock, soothed there, then gently trailed a path up her spine.

Heaven, she accorded simply as she sank in to him and held on.

The room was bathed in a soft glow from dimmed lights, and held a surreal quality.

'Want to talk about it?'

Manolo's voice was low, husky, as his lips skimmed her temple.

'No.' At least not now. Maybe tomorrow. The powerful beat of his heart against her cheek was reassuring. 'You didn't have to come back.'

'Yes,' he said quietly, 'I did. The thought of you suffering harm…' His expression bore the starkness of intense pain. 'It's as well I had to face a long flight,' he opined grimly. 'If I'd arrived on the heels of the police, I'd have torn Roger limb from limb.'

She swallowed the faint lump in her throat.

His hands slowly skimmed the surface of her skin,

outlining her body, the curves, indentations, soothing
with a touch so gentle it made her want to cry.

'I needed to hold you, touch you.'

Was it her imagination, or did his voice sound as
if he was in the grip of some powerful emotion?

'You could have called me.'

The touch of his hands was addictive, seducing
when she doubted they meant to seduce.

'It wouldn't have been enough.'

What was he saying?

'*Madre di Dios.*' The words whispered against the
curve of her mouth. 'Do you have any conception
what I went through when I received Santos' phone
call?'

'He shouldn't have worried you.'

'If he hadn't, his life wouldn't have been worth
living.' He had instant recall of using his cellphone
to call his pilot, then he'd walked out of an important
meeting with the briefest explanation, had a PA arrange a cab to his hotel, where he'd collected his bag
before being driven to the airport.

Once they were airborne, he'd contacted lawyers,
Santos, and done much to restructure his business life.

'From now on, I intend to delegate, split my working time between the city office and home.' He'd also
minimise overseas travel.

Dammit, he had everything he needed right here in
his arms. Anything else faded into insignificance.

The possibility he could have lost the most impor-

tant woman in his life at the hands of a psychotic…
His body trembled at the thought.

Ariane raised her head to look at him, and almost
died at what she saw revealed in his expression. His
eyes…dear heaven, those beautiful dark eyes were
laid bare, mirroring his soul.

She felt as if she was poised on the edge of a prec-
ipice, aware of an emotion so profound she forgot to
breathe.

'Manolo.' His name sighed from her lips with aching wonder, and she blinked back the threat of tears
as his mouth closed over hers in a kiss that was everything she could wish for, all she'd ever wanted
from this man.

It was a kiss that went deep with such a degree of
tendresse it was all she could do not to weep.

'I love you.' They were words he'd never uttered
before. To any woman.

Ariane lifted a hand and touched his cheek, felt the
firm flesh and bone, and trailed her fingertips over the
curve of his mouth.

'Thank you,' she said shakily, and felt his lips
move.

'For loving you?'

'For the ultimate gift.'

This woman, his wife…she undid him, completely.

He showed her what she meant to him as no mere
words could in an oral supplication so incredibly gen-

tle it was all she could do not to cry out. And when she did, he took such care she almost wept.

Afterwards, on the edge of sleep, she curled her hand in his and brought it to her lips. 'You're my life,' she said simply. 'The sun, the moon…stars. Everything. All of it.' She could wait until morning, but she wanted it said now. 'You gave me back the strength to trust again. And taught me what love should be.' There was more, so much more.

'I agreed to be your wife, for the very reasons you offered me marriage. You gave me the chance to share your daughter in place of the child I could never have. For that alone I would pledge my affection, my loyalty for a lifetime.' She paused, searching for the right words. 'I didn't want to fall in love with you.'

'But you did, anyway?' Manolo teased gently.

An impish smile curved her mouth. 'It was your irresistible charm.'

His deep chuckle threatened to break into outright laughter. 'Charm, huh?'

'This is supposed to be a serious moment,' Ariane chided, appeased as he transferred their linked hands and nuzzled her knuckles.

'Believe I'm very serious,' he assured.

At the witching hour of midnight it seemed the right time for confidences and truth. 'Christina's mother,' Ariane ventured quietly.

Manolo told her, all of it. The duplicity, the DNA, the marriage deal, the pay-off. 'Christina is my daughter,' he said with heartfelt simplicity. 'And I get to keep what is mine.'

Ariane pressed her lips to his shoulder.

'For the record,' he added huskily, 'Valentina was never an intimate part of my life.'

It was all she wanted to hear, everything she needed to remove every last skerrick of doubt.

A snuffling cry sounded through the baby monitor, and was quickly followed by another.

'I'll go check.' Manolo slid from the bed and caught up a robe.

'We both will,' Ariane declared, following his actions.

Christina stopped crying the instant they entered the nursery, only to push a fist against her mouth and begin crying again.

'I'll change her nappy.' Manolo crossed to the cupboard and retrieved one, then tended to the replacement.

'I think she's getting another tooth.' Ariane traced a finger over the tiny gums and was rewarded with a wail. 'Poor sweetheart,' she soothed, reaching for the teething gel. 'Let's see if this helps, hmm?'

Between the gel and a pacifier, Christina was soon lulled back to sleep, and they quietly returned to their own suite.

'She's going to grow into a beautiful young woman,' Ariane predicted as she shed her robe.

'With you as her mother, how could she not acquire your values, your integrity?'

She felt her bones begin to melt. 'A compliment?'

'Get used to it.' He shucked off his robe and slid into bed.

'I love you.' The words were quietly spoken, from the heart, and robbed the breath from his throat as he saw the emotion evident in her expressive features.

It took a moment to locate his voice. 'I know it.'

Ariane slid in beside him. 'Is that all you have to say?' she teased, sure of him in a way she had never thought to be.

Manolo pulled her close, sliding one hand down to cup her buttocks as he tunnelled his fingers through her hair to hold fast her nape. 'You need words, *amante*?'

No, she didn't. He proved how much she meant to him each day, every night in the look, his touch, the way his heart beat faster whenever she came close.

'Words would be nice.'

His lips brushed against hers, savoured briefly, then slid up to rest at her temple. 'You're my life,' he said simply.

She felt as if she would melt, and she wrapped her arms around him and held on.

'Everything I ever wanted, and thought I'd never have,' he continued gently.

She was going to cry. Emotion welled up inside and threatened to break her control.

'Beautiful.' His mouth slid down to cover hers in a kiss that was sensuously evocative, and she lost herself in it for a while, then groaned a little when he lifted his head. 'In the heart, where it counts.'

Ariane pulled his mouth down to hers. 'You don't play fair.' And kissed him back with a passion he matched and surpassed.

There was no doubt where this was leading, or how it would end. For now, it was the enjoyment of the journey.

'You want more?' Manolo queried, amused, and suffered the edges of her teeth.

'You.' She soothed the bite with the tip of her tongue. 'Just you.'

'*Querida*,' he said gently, 'that's a given.'

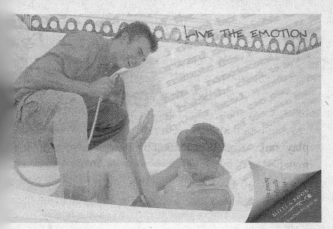

LIVE THE EMOTION

Modern
romance™

...international affairs
– seduction and
passion guaranteed

Medical
romance™

...pulse-raising
romance – heart-
racing medical drama

Tender
romance™

...sparkling, emotional,
feel-good romance

Sensual
romance™

...teasing, tempting,
provocatively playful

Historical
romance™

...rich, vivid and
passionate

Blaze™

...scorching hot
sexy reads

27 new titles every month.

Live the emotion

MILLS & BOON®

MB5

MILLS & BOON®

Live the emotion

Modern
romance™

MISTRESS OF CONVENIENCE by Penny Jordan

Suzy has never been called a security risk before – but
Colonel Lucas Soames insists she is. In order to safeguard
his top secret mission, the suave millionaire forces her to
pose as his mistress. Secreted away in a luxurious Italian
villa it isn't long before their attraction reaches boiling
point…

THE PASSIONATE HUSBAND by Helen Brooks

Marsha Kane is shocked to see her soon-to-be ex-husband
again. She hasn't seen Taylor since she left him for
cheating on her; now she's trying desperately not to fall
for him all over again. Taylor is determined to get Marsha
back – and he always gets what he wants…doesn't he?

HIS BID FOR A BRIDE by Carole Mortimer

Skye O'Hara's life is rocked by tragedy and she's reunited
with Falkner Harrington – her father's enigmatic business
partner. Needing some time to adjust, she accepts when
Falkner offers her the sanctuary of his home. However,
Skye soon suspects that he has a secret agenda…

THE BRABANTI BABY by Catherine Spencer

Gabriel Brabanti wants to see the baby he's been told is
his daughter – but not his ex-wife. So Eve Caldwell
arrives at his Maltese villa with the child. Eve captivates
him – but Gabriel is convinced she's lying. Eve leaves
Gabriel's house, and his bed, but her heart is breaking…

On sale 6th August 2004

*Available at most branches of WHSmith, Tesco, Martins, Borders,
Eason, Sainsbury's and all good paperback bookshops.*

0704/01a

MILLS & BOON®

Live the emotion

Modern
romance™

THE ITALIAN TYCOON'S MISTRESS by *Cathy Williams*

When tycoon Rocco Losi takes over Losi Construction he
tries to sack Amy Hogan. But his belief that she'll leave
quietly is soon challenged – by Amy! Who is this little
spitfire who thinks she can out-argue him – and turn him
on? Rocco decides that Amy can stay after all...

THE GREEK'S SEVEN DAY SEDUCTION by *Susan Stephens*

When Charlotte joined in a dance traditionally performed
only by men – she didn't expect Iannis Kiriakos's
passionate reaction! She can't resist the incredible sexual
current flowing between them, so why not indulge in a
holiday? But she has no idea who Iannis really is...

THE SHEIKH'S BARTERED BRIDE by *Lucy Monroe*

After a whirlwind courtship, Sheikh Hakim bin Omar al
Kadar proposes marriage. Shy, innocent Catherine
Benning has fallen head-over-heels in love, and accepts.
After the wedding they travel to Hakim's desert kingdom
– and Catherine discovers that Hakim has bought her!

BY ROYAL COMMAND by *Robyn Donald*

Lauren's only escape from the war-torn island of
Sant'Rosa is to marry Guy, a total stranger, in a fake
ceremony. Later, reunited with Guy, Lauren is
overwhelmed by an explosive desire. But Guy has news
for her. Their marriage vows were legal and, what's more,
he's really a prince...

On sale 6th August 2004

*Available at most branches of WHSmith, Tesco, Martins, Borders,
Eason, Sainsbury's and all good paperback bookshops.*

4 FREE

books and a surprise gift!

We would like to take this opportunity to thank you for reading t
Mills & Boon® book by offering you the chance to take FOU
more specially selected titles from the Modern Romance™ ser
absolutely FREE! We're also making this offer to introduce you
the benefits of the Reader Service™—

- ★ FREE home delivery
- ★ FREE gifts and competitions
- ★ FREE monthly Newsletter
- ★ Exclusive Reader Service offers
- ★ Books available before they're in the shops

Accepting these FREE books and gift places you under
obligation to buy, you may cancel at any time, even after receivi
your free shipment. Simply complete your details below and retu
the entire page to the address below. *You don't even need a stamp*

YES! Please send me 4 free Modern Romance books and
surprise gift. I understand that unless you hear from me
will receive 6 superb new titles every month for just £2.69 eac
postage and packing free. I am under no obligation to purchase a
books and may cancel my subscription at any time. The free boo
and gift will be mine to keep in any case.

P4Z

Ms/Mrs/Miss/Mr ....Initials.............................
BLOCK CAPITALS PLEA

Surname ....

Address ....

....

....Postcode.............................

Send this whole page to:
UK: FREEPOST CN81, Croydon, CR9 3WZ
EIRE: PO Box 4546, Kilcock, County Kildare (stamp required)